The Song of Vengeance

Dybbuk Scrolls Trilogy
Book 2

By
Alisse Lee Goldenberg

pandamoon
publishing

www.pandamoonpublishing.com

Jacket design and illustrations © Pandamoon Publishing
Art Direction by Don Kramer: Pandamoon Publishing
Editing by Zara Kramer, Rachel Schoenbauer, Heather Stewart, and Genevieve Taylor: Pandamoon Publishing

Pandamoon Publishing and the portrayal of a panda and a moon are registered trademarks of Pandamoon Publishing.

Edition: 2, ver 2.00

ISBN-10: 1-945502-63-0
ISBN-13: 978-1-945502-63-7

Dedication

To my husband Brian and our wonderful children.

Friends are the mirror, reflecting the truth of who we are.
-Yiddish proverb

The Song of Vengeance

Prologue

"Are you certain this plan of yours will work?" The dybbuk's voice was rough with anger.

"I am certain." The man bowed to the dybbuk. He was trembling from head to toe. His shirt was stained with sweat. The brown hair of his beard was matted from all the nervous tugging he had been doing.

"How can this be?" the dybbuk asked him. His yellow eyes flashed, and he grinned, showing a mouth filled with sharp teeth. The dybbuk sat perched on the edge of his seat, buzzing with energy. "All the ways between worlds have been sealed."

"That would be impossible," the man said. He looked up in fear to see if his comment had angered the dybbuk. He knew how they hated being contradicted. "There are far too many ways for people to cross over for anyone to seal them all. I have found one that you can use for your purposes."

"Good," the dybbuk said. He rubbed his gnarled hands together excitedly. "It has been over a year now. High time for those girls to pay the price for what they did to our king. Your idea is the perfect for this. Our revenge will be sweet."

The man saw two other dybbuks emerge from the shadows, feral grins on their faces. Their yellow eyes glowed in the darkness of what was once Asmodeus' throne room. He trembled with fear.

"Remember our bargain," the man said, struggling to keep his voice steady. He was pleased to find that he had succeeded. Too much was riding on his being taken seriously. "You keep your end of it, and I will keep mine. You will not hurt a single hair on my child's head."

"Do not be afraid," the dybbuk said to him. "We always keep our word. You will be greatly rewarded for your service to us. I promised you this—and a dybbuk never breaks any promise given. A bargain is a bargain." He turned to the others. "He will show you the way. Follow our servant and do as he says. Our time is now. Vengeance will finally be ours."

The two dybbuks by his side nodded and followed the man out of the room.

"These mortals are too easy to control," he said to himself. He chuckled, a low gravelly sound emanating from the back of his throat. "Soon I shall have all I seek: revenge, power, a title all of my own. This fool will make all of this possible, and I shall see him on his knees before me, groveling to his lord and master," the man heard the dybbuk say from his seat on the throne. The dybbuk's words sent a chill through his heart as he walked on out of the room.

Chapter One:
Chaverim Nedarim

Carrie sat at her desk, her brow creased in concentration. She had been trying for hours to not give in to the distractions of social media, or the desire to call her friends. She had far too much to do, and increasingly little time to finish it in. She looked over what she had written so far, her lips pursed as she perused her words.

William Shakespeare's play Romeo and Juliet *is considered by many to be the pinnacle work of fiction in the romantic tragedy genre. However, when one looks closer at what is said and what is shown on stage, it has clearly been misrepresented.* Romeo and Juliet *is not the tragedy people see it to be. In fact, William Shakespeare's play is a masterpiece of a parody of the romantic tragedies of the day. It is rife with comedy; from Romeo's infatuation with Rosaline, to the fake suicide and miscommunications...*

Carrie took her hands off her keyboard, sighed in frustration, and pushed herself away from her desk. Why she had chosen this topic for her paper? Why was she even taking this course? Most importantly, why couldn't she just run out the door and be on her way to visit Lindsay and Rebecca? Despite their best efforts, the three friends had not been able to find a university with programs that suited all of their needs. They had originally thought they would study folklore, but over the course of their last year of high school, it had soon become clear that such a program was not suited to either Lindsay or Carrie. Lindsay had far too much of a desire to perform, and Carrie was still having trouble making up her mind. It had been an anguished summer where they spent as much time as possible together knowing they would part in the fall. The desire to call them again mounted with her frustration.

Carrie, Lindsay, and Rebecca had always been best friends. They had been inseparable since the age of three. Luck had placed them in the same classes at school virtually every year. When they had gone to summer camp, they were always in the same cabin. Now, at the age of eighteen, they were apart for the first time. Carrie had gone to York University and had begun studying Psychology, yet soon realized the program was not for her. Now she was undecided in her major and seriously questioning the direction her life was taking. She wished she was as focused as her friends. Lindsay was studying performance at the Berklee School of Music all the way in Boston. Rebecca was in Ottawa studying literature with a focus on folklore. Both of her friends seemed to know exactly what they wanted and how to get it. Despite the adventures they had had not too long ago, Carrie felt more adrift than ever before, and she had no idea as to how to fix it. She looked down at her desk; sitting next to her computer were two small gift boxes. Both of her friends had birthdays coming up, and Carrie had their gifts ready. She had bought them both silver filigree *chamtzahs* and could not wait to give them to them.

Carrie looked around her tiny room and wondered where she had put her phone. It always seemed to be lost. One of these days, she was going to have to duct tape it to her hand to prevent it from vanishing. As she looked, her gaze fell on a small collection of watercolor paintings that were taped up on the wall by her bed. Carrie had begun painting them soon after she and her friends had returned from their travels in Hadariah. In one, she could see the smiling face of Joldisch Riz. In another, she saw Emilia smiling in the light blue dress she had worn at the celebratory feast. However, the majority of the paintings were a memorial to Adom, the fox. In one, Adom was running from Finnigan in Carrie's backyard. In another, Adom was staring out of the piece of paper, a quizzical smile on his face. In a third, Adom had a thoughtful expression while sitting atop a rock in a dark forest clearing. Carrie sighed and resumed her search for her phone. She tossed clothes off of her bed, unsure of whether or not they were clean or dirty, and smiled when she saw the handset half-under her pillow. Her eyes shone as she punched in Lindsay's cell phone number. It had been a week since either of her friends had spoken with her, and she was getting a little antsy. This was unusual for them, as they usually spoke daily. This was the longest they had gone without any form of communication whatsoever.

"Hi! You've reached Lindsay," Carrie heard as her friend's voicemail picked up. "I'm clearly not here, or I'm avoiding your call. Leave a message, and if I remember to check voicemail, I might call you back."

Carrie smiled. She could just see the tiny blonde bouncing around her room as she recorded the message. "Hi, Lindsay," Carrie said into her phone. "It's Carrie. Um, call me?" She grimaced as she hung up. She hated leaving voicemail. It didn't matter who it was for. She always felt so awkward and never seemed to know what to say. She looked at her phone and sighed once more. She dialled Rebecca. Maybe her other friend would be around to talk.

Rebecca's voicemail picked up on the third ring. "Hi, you've reached Rebecca. Leave a message at the beep."

Carrie left a message for Rebecca to call her back and returned to her desk. She supposed that she should finish her essay. It was due for the next class, and she had only managed to write the first paragraph. A knock on the door quickly brought her out of her musings.

"Hey, Carrie," a voice said.

Carrie looked up to see her neighbour Amanda standing at the door of her room. "Hey," Carrie answered.

"A group of us are going to Shopsey's. Wanna come?" Amanda asked. She pulled a hair elastic out of her pocket and pulled her brown hair into a ponytail. Her purple glasses glinted in the light from Carrie's lamp.

"Sure," Carrie said. Her essay could wait. She needed to get out and be with people tonight. She stood and grabbed a sweatshirt from her bed. Pulling it on, she walked over to join Amanda in the hall. "Let's go."

Carrie pulled her key from her pocket and locked her room. Her friends would call back soon. She was sure of that. They were just busy. She could relate to that all too well. Even though her marks were good, she had not been prepared for the sheer amount of note taking and reading that university would require her to do. While in high school, it had taken them months to read Hamlet; in her Shakespeare course, they had breezed through it in a week. She definitely needed this time away from her computer screen.

* * *

Carrie sat at a table, absently stirring her coffee and trying to follow the different threads of conversation swirling around her. Amanda and an animated young man named Mike were cheerily dissecting her TA's inability to put together an outfit. Beside them, two dance majors were talking about multiple choice tests and the importance of the "when in doubt, choose 'C'" method while a film major was arguing vociferously with them.

Carrie liked these people. However, tonight she was content to just sit and listen. She took a sip of her coffee and smiled as Mike made Amanda laugh loudly at his description of a particularly awful pink paisley top. She knew Amanda liked him, but she could also tell her neighbour was not his type. Carrie looked at her watch and grimaced as she saw how late it had gotten. She really needed to get that paper finished.

"Excuse me," Carrie said as she rose from the table. "I've really got to go. I have a paper due tomorrow."

"Come on," Mike said. "Can't you stay a bit longer?"

"I only wrote the first paragraph," Carrie explained. "It's only half-researched. I really need to get it finished. With everything I've still got to do here, I doubt I'll get any sleep tonight."

"Go," Mike said, wincing in sympathy. "Do what you gotta do. All-nighters suck."

"They sure do," Carrie said. "See you guys soon."

"Good luck with your paper," Amanda said, waving goodbye.

Carrie walked the short distance back to her residence in the Vanier College building. Despite the small size of the rooms, she actually liked that it was in one of the older buildings on the university campus. She liked the feeling of history that was in the halls filled with pictures of over fifty years of graduating students. Her parents had objected to her moving onto campus. They had argued that she lived close enough to the university to commute, but she wanted the experience of living where she went to school. She didn't want to feel like she was missing out on anything. In the end, they had finally relented.

As she walked, Carrie pulled her arms around her chest, hugging herself protectively. The nights were starting to take on an early winter chill. Most of the trees had already lost their leaves. She was a short distance from the college's doorway when she felt the familiar prickling on the back of her neck. It had been over a year since she had felt it. A year since she, Lindsay, and Rebecca had returned from their quest in Hadariah. A year of her searching futilely for another way back into that magical land. Nothing had worked.

Carrie stopped walking. She could feel her heart pounding in her chest. Her breath quickened. She looked around, trying to see what was causing this feeling. A flash of red darted past her and went into a small bush to her right.

"Adom?" Carrie whispered. She instantly chided herself for being foolish. Her eyes prickled with tears. She knew that could not be possible. Adom was gone. She had been there when he had died. The chaos of the throne room, the pain and horror of that day still filled her dreams. However, with the strange feeling coupled with that flash, she thought that just maybe, there might be a chance. Carrie willed her legs to walk over to the bush, and she crouched down, trying to peer into the inky blackness between its branches. Nothing was there. The prickling feeling intensified on the back of her neck. Carrie quickly stood up and turned to look behind her. Just out of the light, Carrie could see a tall shape standing on a small hill. Carrie could not see him clearly, but she was certain that they were staring right at her.

"Hello?" Carrie said. "Can I help you?" She squinted into the darkness, trying to see who it was.

At the sound of her voice, the figure turned and quickly walked away. Carrie shuddered and entered her building. The feeling was gone from her body. She went up to her residence, trying hard to forget what had just happened. She had a paper to write.

Chapter Two:
Eyfo Aten?

Carrie woke up with a start. She groaned and rolled over to where her alarm clock lay blaring. Slapping the snooze button, she swore loudly as she looked at the time. The alarm must have been going off for a while before she had finally heard it. Carrie leapt out of bed and quickly began throwing on clothes. She ran down the hall to the shared bathroom, forgoing most of her morning routine as she tried to get ready as quickly as possible.

Carrie was halfway to Vari Hall when she stopped short, realizing she had left the paper she had slaved over all through the night sitting on her desk. Muttering under her breath, in language that would make the most seasoned sailor blush, Carrie turned and ran back to her room as fast as her legs could carry her. This was not her day.

Finally easing herself into a desk in the classroom, Carrie allowed herself to catch her breath. Sam, the young man leading the tutorial, nodded in her direction, his floppy brown hair falling into his eyes as he did so. Carrie could swear that his disapproval of her tardiness was written all over his features. She managed to get a notebook, pen, and her single volume collection of Shakespeare's plays out of her bag with as little noise as possible and willed herself into invisibility. Carrie's stomach rumbled, and she wondered if she could grab a granola bar out of her bag and eat it without attracting Sam's attention, but thought it might not be the best idea. She was already in trouble for being late. She didn't want to make things any worse for herself.

Carrie had just settled into her routine of taking notes as Sam spoke about Shakespeare's use of imagery and pathetic fallacy to further emphasize the themes of his plays when she felt it again. That familiar prickling wound its way up the back of Carrie's neck, like the charge felt in the air before a violent storm. It was stronger now than it had been the night before.

Carrie looked up and gazed around the classroom. Her eyes settled on a stranger. The tutorial was a small group, and Carrie knew everyone in it. If not by name, then by sight. She was certain that this boy had not been in the class before. Her eyes narrowed as she examined him. Even sitting, he looked quite tall. His knees nearly touched the bottom of his desk, and he was exceedingly thin. His hair was black, cropped short, and had a slight curl to it. His light-coloured eyes were almost too large for his face, his nose too small. His mouth was very wide with thin lips that seemed set in a look of concentration.

Everything about him seemed slightly off. He had no notebook, no laptop, no way of taking notes. His hands were placed on top of the desk, long fingers moving restlessly, as if tracing some intricate pattern. His clothes seemed too crisp, too clean, white button-down shirt tucked into stiff, dark jeans. Carrie instinctively looked around him to see if he cast a shadow, and was surprised to find that he did. Next to him, Carrie felt positively dowdy in her sweats, and she was embarrassed to note that in her haste that morning, she had grabbed two completely mismatched socks.

Aside from this boy, Carrie could see nothing else odd around the room. She could not see how or why, but she was certain the strange feeling was coming from him. It wasn't odd for some students to bring a friend to check out a class, or for someone to listen in. The TAs allowed it, and the professors didn't mind as long as they weren't disruptive, but this boy seemed alone.

The rest of the tutorial seemed to pass by in a blur. Carrie was only half-listening to the discussion being led. When Sam ended the class, Carrie dropped her paper on his desk and apologized for being late before high-tailing it out of the room, determined to speak to the mysterious boy who had caught her eye. However, when she entered the main hallway, he was nowhere to be found. Frustrated, Carrie set off to return to her room.

* * *

Carrie stared at her phone in frustration. The two people she could openly speak to about this were both not answering her calls. She had tried emailing them, texting them, sending them every kind of message she could think of, and had heard nothing back. Resentfully, she wondered if it was because both of her friends had started seeing people at their schools. Lindsay had started dating her costar Bradley from her upcoming community theatre production of *Chess*. She had sent Carrie pictures of the two of them together, and they seemed happy. Rebecca had begun seeing a boy named Ryan she had met in a class she was taking on Greek Civilizations. She seemed very happy with the way things were going. Just as quickly as it had come upon her, Carrie dismissed this train of thought. All three of them had gone out with boys before, and it had never come between them in the past. There was no reason it should be a problem now. She sighed and threw her phone across the room so it landed on her bed. Carrie looked at the framed picture of the three of them sitting on her desk. It was taken the day before their first year of university started. Carrie, Lindsay, and Rebecca were sitting on Carrie's back porch. Carrie's sandy hair had grown from her usual pixie cut into a shaggy bob that just skimmed her chin. Her blue-green eyes twinkled in the late summer sun. Lindsay was wearing a loud, pink dress. Her long blonde hair had been cut into a layered shoulder-length style. Her petite frame was tiny compared to Rebecca's tall silhouette. Rebecca's straight dark hair was pulled back, and she seemed relaxed and happy.

Carrie could not think of a single plausible reason her two best friends could be avoiding her. She got up and retrieved her phone. Her mom picked up on the second ring.

"Honey?" Her mom sounded concerned. "You never call at this time of day. What's going on?"

"Hey, Mom," Carrie said. "How's Finn?"

"He's doing well," her mom replied. "We took him to the vet the other day for his yearly checkup, and he's old, but happy. But I'm assuming you didn't call to ask about your dog."

Carrie smiled. Her mother knew her so well. "No, I guess I'm a little homesick," she told her.

"You can always come home," her mom said. "You don't have to stay in residence."

"I know," Carrie said. In the background, she could hear the vacuum cleaner going in her parents' house. She smiled, picturing her dad cleaning up. "I like it here though. I'm having fun, meeting new people. I guess I'm a little bummed that Lindsay and Rebecca aren't returning my calls."

"Who?" her mom asked. "Can we talk later? I'm having trouble hearing you. Your father's cleaning a mess he made. He knocked over one of my plants. Soil's everywhere."

"Okay," Carrie answered. "I love you, Mom."

"Love you, too, sweetie," her mother said as she hung up the phone.

Carrie was at a loss. Though nothing weird had been said, the conversation with her mom left her feeling a little strange. The events of the past few days were so odd. At least the last time her life had taken such a turn she had not felt so alone. When Adom had approached her that summer, she had had the support of her friends. She had had someone there for her, someone to talk to. Now, she didn't know which way to turn. Just thinking of Adom made her ache inside. Carrie thought back to the night before. She was so certain she had seen something small and red run into that bush. But Adom was gone. She knew that with great certainty. She had held him in her arms, and she had been there when he died. There was no coming back from that. So what had that been? Another fox? Furthermore, that dark shape she had seen watching her had not appeared particularly friendly.

Carrie spun in her desk chair feeling frustrated and confused. She did not like being in the dark about things. She wanted answers. She wanted someone to talk this out with.

"Hey there," Amanda said as she poked her head into the room. "I hope you don't mind my coming in here. Your door was open."

Carrie smiled at her. "No problem," she said. "What's up?"

Amanda entered fully and looked closely at Carrie. "You okay?" she asked. "You seem a bit distracted."

"Sorry," Carrie replied. "I've just been trying to reach my friends now for over a week. No one's picking up their phones or answering any of my messages. It's a bit annoying."

"Oh," Amanda said. "Do I know these friends of yours? Want me to go shake 'em down for being jerks?"

"You're so weird." Carrie smiled. "No, I told you about them. Lindsay and Rebecca. They went away to school I stayed here. I'm sure it's not a big deal. Probably got busy with school stuff."

Amanda looked thoughtful. "I don't remember you saying anything about them," she said slowly as she cocked her head to the side. "You probably did though." She laughed. "I suck with names. I'm sure they'll call. You're too awesome to ignore. Anyway, just popped in to say 'hi.' So, hi! I've got some reading I'm neglecting. Talk to you later."

Amanda walked out the door leaving Carrie sitting bewildered at her desk. Something was definitely going on, and she hated it. She picked up the picture on her desk. She stared at it for a moment and put it back down forcefully. She stood and walked to her window. A dark figure was standing under a tree looking up to where she was. Carrie gasped. The boy from her class stood there staring, a scowl etched across his features. She reached up and began twisting the gold chain of her chamtzah around her fingers. Somehow, she just knew that look was meant for her.

Chapter Three:
Khaloymes ve Sfeykes

Sunlight trickled in through the leaves in the trees all around her. Carrie tilted her face upward drinking in the rays. A soft smile played across her lips. She took a slow breath in, and her smile widened into a grin as she felt herself relax for the first time in days.

"I missed this place," she said. "I didn't think it would be possible to want to return anywhere so badly, but every day I looked for a way to come back. And now I'm finally here."

"I knew you could do it," Adom said.

Carrie looked down at the small fox who sat whole and well on the log next to her. His button-black eyes looked up at her, filled with pride and a touch of something else. Was it sadness? Carrie's smile faltered.

"You were told that the ways between worlds were plentiful," Adom continued. "It was only a matter of time before you found your way back." He cocked his head to the side and looked at Carrie closely. "What is troubling you?" he asked her.

Carrie took a breath. She had been having such a nice time. She feared talking about her problems would only destroy the relaxed mood she was in. She reached out and lightly stroked Adom's rusty fur. She frowned, wondering where to begin.

"I think I'm being followed," Carrie said. "I'm have this strange feeling coming over me. It feels just like the first couple of times I saw you. Like there's something... I don't know..." she faltered, feeling completely lost.

"Magic?" Adom asked. He put his head in Carrie's lap and curled up against her leg. She was struck by how much he was like her dog, Finnigan.

"Just like magic," Carrie agreed. "But it's not like you. The first couple of times I saw you, I knew you were there before you made yourself known. But I wasn't really afraid. This though...I don't think whatever's doing this is a nice kind of magic. There's this boy in one of my classes. I know he's never been there before. He doesn't take notes. He just sat there last class moving his fingers on his desk. And last night, I saw him outside my residence. He was staring up with an angry expression on his face, and I know he was looking at me. I just know it! And on top of all this, Rebecca and Lindsay won't call me back. I don't know how to even start getting a hold of Emilia to ask her about all this. Can you help me?" Carrie looked earnestly into Adom's eyes. She felt so upset, so helpless.

"You know I can't," Adom sadly replied.

"Why not?" Carrie asked. She winced at how whiny her question sounded. She knew she sounded like a petulant child.

"You know why," Adom answered. He sighed and nuzzled closer against her.

"Surely you know something more than I do," Carrie said.

"I only know as much as you do," Adom said with a note of regret in his voice. "No more, no less."

"But you're magic," Carrie protested. "You have to know something! How can you know nothing?"

"You know why," Adom said again.

Carrie felt her eyes tear up. "You're not real," she said. "You're not really here." She looked around at the forest. "I'm not really here either."

"No," Adom said. "None of this is real."

"But," Carrie said. She shook her head. "How is this possible? I don't understand."

"Yes, you do understand," Adom told her. He stood and turned away. "And now it's time for you to wake up, Carrie." He began to walk deeper into the forest.

Carrie saw the light begin to fade. Everything around her seemed to lose focus. The trees around her seemed to melt into nothingness. She quickly got to her feet. "Adom!" she called after him. "Please don't leave me. I don't want to be alone."

"Trust me," Adom said looking over his shoulder. "You will never be alone."

"I'm sorry," Carrie said. A tear trickled down her cheek.

"I know," Adom answered. He walked into the oncoming darkness and was gone from Carrie's sight.

* * *

Carrie woke up in her room. Her pillow was damp from her tears. She reached up and rubbed a hand over her face. It had all been a dream. She stretched her hand out over to the small table next to her bed and picked up her phone. She looked at the screen. No missed calls. She gritted her teeth and sat up. Her clock read 5:00 a.m. Somehow, she doubted she would be getting any more sleep before she had to be in class that day. She crossed over to her computer and checked her email. Still nothing. The silence from her friends was getting unnerving. She composed an email to them both, telling them about her dream. She told them everything that had happened over the past week. How she had felt she was being watched, all about the odd boy in her class, the red shape that had darted past her and disappeared into the bush. Clicking send, Carrie sat back in her chair and took a deep breath. Even just writing it all out and sending it made her feel a little better. It wasn't nearly as good as the give and take of a real conversation, but getting it off her chest had helped. She felt lighter, calmer, as if a weight had been lifted. She stared at her inbox, as if willing a response to appear, but she somehow knew it was not going to happen.

When Carrie, Rebecca, and Lindsay had decided to go to separate schools, they had promised to keep in touch as often as possible. Both Rebecca and Lindsay had come home for holidays and a couple of weekends, and Carrie had been to visit them both as well. There had barely been a day that she had not heard from at least one of them until now.

Standing and walking toward her window, Carrie rolled her head around, trying to ease the tension that remained in her neck. She looked outside at the light layer of frost that lay softly upon the grass. It was unusual for it to be so cold this time of year, but Carrie loved the way the frozen blanket seemed to make the grass sparkle under the lamplight. The sun was barely beginning to peek through the spaces between the buildings on campus, and Carrie was relieved to see there was no one milling about outside. She had been nervous that the boy from before would still be standing there peering up at her window. She smiled to herself; she was being silly. No one would be so crazy as to wait and watch her room while she slept. Would they?

* * *

Later that night, Carrie sat at her desk typing away at yet another paper she had left to the last minute. She was furious with herself. She had never allowed things to get this bad in high school. And yet, here on her own, she felt as if she were drowning. She needed to speak to someone who understood. But her two best friends would not return her calls. She looked at the silent phone sitting beside her and sighed. She picked it up and called home.

"Hello?" Carrie's mother answered on the first ring.

"Hi, Mom," Carrie said with a small smile.

13

"Are you okay? You sound tired."

"Oh, just left a paper too long. I'm fine otherwise," Carrie said.

"You don't have to torture yourself like that," Carrie's mother said.

"I'm fine, Mom," Carrie replied. "I'm just about done." She winced at the lie, knowing she had another twelve pages to go.

"Mmhmm," her mother replied, as if she didn't believe her.

"Mom?" she asked, hearing the disapproval in her mother's voice. "What is it?"

"Are you all right?" her mother enquired. "You seem tired, and a bit…worn," she finished. "I worry about you."

Carrie shrugged off her mother's concern. "I'm fine Mom," she said. "Really. It's just…" she trailed off, unsure of how to finish.

"What is it, honey?" Carrie's mother asked.

"I…" Carrie paused.

"How's school going?" she asked. It was clear from the tone of her voice that she did not mean how her classes were going.

"School's fine," Carrie answered. "I love most of my classes. It's great being able to actually argue with your teachers instead of just nodding and going along with whatever they say. You know?"

"Yes, I imagine that must be a nice change."

"It is."

"How about friends? Are you making any? Do you like living on campus? Are your fellow students nice to you?"

Carrie smiled. "Yes, Mom," she answered. "The girl next door, Amanda, is super nice. We go out for coffees sometimes, hang in each other's rooms. I met all her friends. Some of them are really friendly, good to talk to. I don't think I would've met this many people without living on campus. I'm enjoying it a lot. I just, well, I miss my old friends though." Carrie chewed on her bottom lip; she debated whether or not to tell her parents her concerns about Rebecca and Lindsay.

"Your old friends?" she asked. She sounded confused. "Why would you miss them?"

"Excuse me?" Carrie asked. She felt anger rising in her. "Why wouldn't I? We do everything together. And now, they don't seem to answer any of my calls, or my emails, or anything! It's a bit weird, don't you think? Honestly, I'm kind of worried."

"Honey," her mother jumped in, stemming the flow of words. "Who are you talking about? I thought all your friends went to York with you."

Carrie gaped at her phone. Was she serious? "Not my best friends," she said. "Rebecca and Lindsay went away to school. They're the ones I can't get ahold of, and after what I told you happened that summer we went away…you remember how I told you all about Hadariah, and Emilia… I'm freaking out a bit."

Carrie heard a sharp intake of breath over the phone line. "Lindsay and Rebecca?" her mother asked, a note of worry in her voice.

"Yes," Carrie said, relieved someone seemed as upset as she was.

"Sweetie," she said. "I haven't heard those names in a long time. Are you sure you're okay?"

"What are you talking about?" Carrie asked. A sinking feeling started to spread through her stomach. She felt queasy, unsure she wanted her mother to answer her question.

"Carrie," her mother continued. "Lindsay and Rebecca, well, what do you remember about them? When was the last time you saw them?"

Carrie swallowed heavily; her mouth was dry. "I—I—" she stuttered. "Rebecca came to visit three weeks ago. I Skyped with Lindsay a week and a half ago. Why?"

"Honey," she said. She sounded upset. "Rebecca and Lindsay aren't real."

"What?" Carrie gasped. Her ears were ringing. She was certain she had heard wrong.

"They're not real," her mother insisted. "They're imaginary."

"You're lying!" Carrie angrily exclaimed. She felt a rush of fear as she realized that something had gotten to her parents. Something was very wrong.

"We haven't heard you use those names in years, sweetheart," she said. "You had two imaginary friends in kindergarten. You called them Rebecca and Lindsay, and you went everywhere with them. We were getting worried because you wouldn't play with any of the other children. Then one day, it just stopped. We were so relieved. What happened to make them come back? Why do you need them now? Are you sure you're okay living on your own? Is this loneliness? Did something happen to you at school? Are you too stressed out?"

"No! I'm not stressed out!" Carrie exclaimed. She swallowed, realizing how absurd that sounded. "I—I have to go."

"Carrie, please talk to me," her mother said.

Carrie looked at the phone in her hand, tears in her eyes. She let out a shaky breath, and put it back to her ear. "I'm fine. Maybe I am a little overworked. I really need to stop leaving these papers to the last minute. I probably need sleep or something." She closed her eyes, feeling tears roll down her cheeks. Her mother couldn't help her. She didn't know if anyone could. "I love you, Mom," she whispered and hung up the phone, cutting off her mom's reply.

Chapter Four:
Tsayt Meshugas

Carrie walked into her room in a daze. Her mind was reeling as she heavily sat down on her bed. How could any of this be happening? It was too cruel for it to be a joke. Besides which, her parents were the last people on earth who would try to trick her like this. Carrie reached for her phone, and with a shaky hand she dialled Lindsay's number, willing her friend to pick up the phone. As she waited for the call to connect, she pictured how they would both laugh over this when they spoke.

"The number you are dialling is not in service. This is a recording—"

Carrie felt numb as she hung up. She tried Rebecca and got the same irritating automated message. She threw her phone down and glared at it, as if blaming it for her predicament. Her friends' number were in her phonebook. Unless there was some glitch, but she knew that was not the case. She knew she was not crazy. There was no way she had made up her two best friends. Everything they had done together was firmly implanted in her memories. Every private joke, every silly thing, every hard time, fight, and adventure was there. She could not possibly have done those things with people who did not exist.

Carrie pondered what she should do next. She picked up the phone once more and dialled Lindsay's home. Mrs. Smith picked up after the third ring.

"Mrs. Smith?" Carrie asked.

"Yes?" answered the warm, familiar voice. "Who is this?"

"It's Carrie. Carrie Eisen."

"Who?" Mrs. Smith said. She sounded confused.

"Your daughter Lindsay's friend," Carrie said. Her heart pounded painfully in her chest. She knew what Lindsay's mother was about to say and did not want to hear it.

"I don't have a daughter," Mrs. Smith said. "I'm sorry, but I think you have the wrong number."

Carrie hung up the phone without saying another word. She felt dizzy with confusion. She thought hard about her situation. This new, and disturbing, development coupled with the odd feelings and that strange boy, could only mean that something magical was happening. This, she was certain of. Whoever was doing this had been thorough. Disconnecting the phone numbers was new, but she could deal with that. Making parents forget their own children was sinking to a vile new low. Carrie got up and went over to her desk. The photo of the three of them still sat where she had left it. She picked it up and gave her friends a long look. Their smiles seemed to validate Carrie's sanity.

"Are you busy?" said a voice from her doorway.

Carrie spun toward it, startled. Amanda stood there grinning happily.

"Did I scare you?" Amanda asked. "Sorry."

"It's okay," Carrie said. She put the picture back on the desk.

"Who's that?" Amanda asked crossing over to pick up the frame. "Friends of yours? They seem nice."

Carrie was sure that Amanda had met them both when they had come to visit. "They're my friends Rebecca and Lindsay," she answered.

"You've never mentioned them," Amanda casually replied as she put the picture back.

Carrie felt her chest grow tight. Panic began rising again. She *knew* she'd mentioned them. Countless times. It was as if her friends had been erased from existence. She felt as if she had to get out of her room. She reached over and grabbed her purse from where it sat on the desk.

"Going out?" Amanda asked.

"I've got to get to the library," Carrie answered. "I'm so behind in my work."

"Okay," Amanda said. "Wanna grab a coffee first?"

"I really can't let myself get distracted now," Carrie replied. "I have so many papers."

"Suit yourself," Amanda shrugged and left the room. Carrie could hear her calling out an invitation to Mike as she grabbed a sweater and headed out herself.

* * *

Later, Carrie sat amidst an ever-growing stack of books and what felt like an even larger pile of notes, many of which were conflicting. She was certain that whatever had happened to her friends had something to do with what had occurred between them and Asmodeus that summer. Now she just had to prove it. Carrie shuffled through her notes trying to decide what to do. She had sheets with notes on possession, mirrors, exorcism, creatures—all manner of things that seemed, at best, complicated and at worst, dangerous. Carrie groaned and put her head down on top of her pile of notes. She ran her hands through her hair and just sat there for a while. She did not want to read another word. It would almost be easier to believe the lie being spun around her, and accept being crazy. She hated how truly alone she felt. She fervently wished her friends were with her, and prayed that wherever they were, they were okay and unharmed. She breathed in and out, eyes closed, hoping that somehow, all would soon be well. She almost didn't notice as the dusty smell of the library was taken over by a familiar smell of mildew and decay.

Carrie raised her head with a start. She felt her heart pound painfully in her chest as she looked around in shock. The library had disappeared, and she found herself surrounded by the filthy stone walls of Asmodeus' dungeon.

She could see the fire from the torches flickering on the walls outside her cell door, and by their light, Carrie could just make out the two shapes curled in the corner farthest from her. She squinted trying to see who they were. Carrie could barely see the blonde hair, pink t-shirt, and denim skirt of one and the black ponytail, red sweater, and black pants on the other.

"Lindsay?" Carrie tentatively called. "Rebecca?" Neither figure moved.

Carrie gingerly picked herself up off the floor and made her way over to the corner. She approached the two girls, softly calling out their names. When each call remained unanswered, the sick feeling that had been building in her stomach grew. The closer she got, the more she could see how pale and still they were. When she was close enough to touch them, she cautiously reached out a trembling hand to touch the blonde on the shoulder. Her eyes grew wide as she took in her chalky complexion, skin drawn tight over bone. She let out a shriek as her touch sent the girl falling into the other.

"No!" Carrie yelled in despair as both girls fell to the floor. She watched in horror as their figures exploded in a shower of ash and dust. Carrie fell to her knees, a sob caught in her throat. She stared helpless at the mess around her feet.

"This can't be real," Carrie whispered to herself. She sat with her arms wrapped tightly around her knees, rocking back and forth. "This can't be happening."

"It isn't," spoke a voice.

Carrie quickly raised her head and looked around.

"You need to wake yourself," the voice spoke again. Carrie noted it was deep and male, full of concern; the speaker had an accent, but not one she could place. It didn't sound British and was certainly not French, Spanish, or German. It was almost like an odd amalgamation of them all.

"I can't," Carrie said. "My friends are gone."

"Then we must get them back," the voice answered.

Carrie could feel a warm hand on her shoulder. She lifted her head to find herself back in the library and staring into the light grey eyes of the boy from her Shakespeare class.

Chapter Five:
Ha Shaliach

Carrie violently pushed herself away from the desk and out of the boy's grasp.

"Who are you?" she demanded, her eyes flashing dangerously in his direction.

He reached for her once more, shaking his head. "Not here," he said. "We are too exposed."

Carrie narrowed her eyes. "I'm going nowhere with you," she said. "I was raised not to walk off with strange men, and I don't even know your name." She crossed her arms, her head full of suspicions and doubts.

"Mikhail," he said to her. "Now that you know what I am called, can we please leave?" He looked around the library as if trying to confirm they were in fact alone.

Carrie shook her head. "I don't trust you," she said to him. "So you gave me something to call you. So what? What does that tell me about you? Nothing. For all I know, that's not even your real name. All I know is that my friends have vanished, and everyone around me thinks they weren't even real to begin with. How do I know you're not going to take me somewhere to do the same thing to me?"

"Emilia said you would be suspicious," Mikhail said with a rueful quirk of his upper lip.

"Emilia?" Carrie asked. Her eyes widened. "What does she have to do with this?" The mention of the fiery-haired princess both relieved and confused her further.

Mikhail looked around, scanning the racks some more. "I told you," he insisted. "Not here."

Carrie gave Mikhail a considering look. "Prove you're on my side."

Mikhail pursed his lips. "I don't see how I can achieve this," he said.

"Try," Carrie said. She felt some pride that she didn't sound as nervous as she felt.

"Emilia told me she was the one who returned your chamtzah to you," Mikhail said, "She also told me she owes her very life to you and your missing friends. She told me how you saved her in her father's cell by giving her that potion made from the enchanted leaves."

Carrie nodded. "Okay," she said slowly. She took a moment to ponder this revelation. She had only told her friends about that. They had been the only ones in that cell. She considered her options. She supposed that Lindsay and Rebecca could have been forced to tell him, and that idea made her shudder. She saw him watching her, his expression carefully neutral. She wanted to send him away, but her desire for information won out. "I don't know if I can trust you, but I need to know what you know." She rose and collected her notes. "Let's go." She turned and led the way out of the library. She hoped she was making the right decision.

* * *

Carrie sat on her bed, staring at Mikhail as he perched on the edge of her desk chair. She stared hard at him and watched as he silently gave her and the mess of her room a long, hard once-over.

"So," Carrie began, breaking the silence. "I took you somewhere else. Talk."

Mikhail nodded toward her open door. "Must this remain so?"

"Yes," Carrie firmly responded.

"All right," he said. "I will tell you what has happened. Since you and your companions defeated Asmodeus, the dybbuks have been in chaos. Without their king, they have been competing for the role of their ruler. When one band has been subdued, another five seem to take its place. The one thing they seem to all agree upon is revenge on you and your friends for Asmodeus' fall from power."

Carrie tightened her lips. Already, she feared where this was heading. "Are the dybbuks responsible for Rebecca and Lindsay disappearing?"

"Yes," Mikhail answered. "When we realized that we would be having trouble with them, the king and queen sealed off the ways between our worlds. Emilia wanted to get word to you, but she was not permitted to do so. It took the dybbuks all this time to find a way to get to you. Emilia sent me to try to stop them. Alas, I was too late to stop them from taking Rebecca and Lindsay, but I resolved to at least save you. I have been following you and casting spells to strengthen the protection of the charm around your neck."

Carrie could feel the acid taste of fury rise in her throat. "Do you have any idea how creepy that is?" she spat out. She was outraged. She had never felt so violated.

Mikhail looked taken aback. "I beg your pardon?" he asked.

"You've known I was in danger for over a week now," Carrie said. She tried to keep from shouting at him. "Instead of doing the right thing by letting me know, you pretty much stalked me, kept me in the dark, and let me go out of my mind worrying about my friends. My parents nearly made me think I was going insane. They think I made Lindsay and Rebecca up. That they're not real. Did you know that?" Carrie balled her hands into tight fists. "I'm not fragile. I'm not going to fall to pieces if you tell me, 'The dybbuks are pissed off that you stopped their king, so they're after you.' I deserve to know what's going on. This *directly* affects me. I am hurt, angry, and highly irritated that you and Emilia decided to keep this from me. You can tell her so. In fact," Carrie paused and looked Mikhail right in the eye. "You can take me to her so I can tell her myself."

Mikhail shook his head. He looked deeply embarrassed, as if Carrie's words had hit home. "I cannot take you to her." he said.

"Why not?" Carrie challenged.

"It was decided that it would be safer for you to stay in your own world," Mikhail told her.

"A fat lot of good that did my friends," Carrie said bitterly. "Whoever made this decision is a total idiot."

"I am truly sorry I did not get to them in time," Mikhail said, his eyes downcast. "Believe me when I say that I did all I could."

Carrie could see from the slump of his shoulders, the way his hands dangled listlessly off the arms of the chair, and the pleading look in his eyes that he was being honest with her in that at least. She felt bad for getting so upset with him, yet she knew she was right to do so. She hated being angry with anyone, almost as much as she hated the idea of people being angry with her.

"So you're saying that this past year, there was no way for my friends and me to return to your world," Carrie said. Finally, it made sense. The king had told them that there were many ways to get to Hadariah, but no matter how hard she, Rebecca, and Lindsay had looked, no way could be found.

Mikhail nodded. "It was thought that this would be best for all," he said. "At least until some way could be found to control the dybbuks who sought to cause harm."

"If it was the dybbuks who took my friends…" Carrie's voice trailed off. A vision of the crumbling bodies from her dream rose unbidden to her mind. She shuddered. And yet, she felt she had to know. "Is there still hope for them?" she asked in a small voice. "It's been days. Are they all right? Where have they taken them?"

"I cannot answer these questions," Mikhail said. "I am so sorry. Emilia believes there is still hope. She does not think those that took your friends will have harmed them yet. She feels they will wait until they have you as well."

Carrie absorbed this information. It made sense to her. It would be the ultimate revenge to force her to bear witness to whatever it was they had in store for Lindsay and Rebecca.

"How do we get them back?" she asked.

"We do not do anything," Mikhail said. "We stay here, where I will help keep you safe, and Emilia works with the king and queen of Hadariah to find your friends."

Carrie swore under her breath. He was being so stubborn. She looked up at him. "You can stay here all you want," she said. "You're forgetting I faced Asmodeus. I'm still here. He isn't. I have every intention of going after the creeps that took my friends. You don't have to help me if you're too scared."

"Fear has nothing to do with it," Mikhail told her. "I swore to Emilia that I would keep you safe and here."

Carrie let her gaze wander until it fell on the picture on her desk. "How do you know Emilia?" she asked.

"She and I have been close friends since early childhood," Mikhail answered.

"You're not a dybbuk," Carrie said. "I saw that you have a shadow."

"No," Mikhail agreed. "I'm not. You are quite observant."

"So how did you meet?" Carrie asked.

"My family lives in the village next to the Mountain of Darkness," Mikhail said. "My father is a farmer. He owns the orchard close by."

Carrie nodded remembering the trees laden with fruit. "He keeps a beautiful farm," she said. "I remember it."

"Thank you," Mikhail said with a small smile. "When I was a young boy, my father took me to pick apples with him. I remember a young girl, she seemed my age, hiding up in one of the trees. I asked her to come down, and she leapt out of the branches, almost seeming to take flight. Rather than be frightened, I laughed. She landed next to me and introduced herself. We have been close friends ever since. She has often had to sneak out of the castle to see me, but we have managed. My father loves her almost as his own daughter. We are more brother and sister than friends now."

"What does your mother think of her?" Carrie asked. She noticed he didn't mention her.

"She died before I met Emilia," Mikhail said.

"I am so sorry," Carrie said. She did not know what she would do without her mother's love and guidance.

"Thank you," he replied.

"I have to ask," Carrie began. "If you were me, and it was Emilia who had been taken and you didn't know if she were alive or dead, would you sit around in your room twiddling your thumbs? Or would you get off your butt and do anything in your power to find her regardless of how dangerous it might be?"

Mikhail sighed. "I understand your feelings," he said.

"But—" Carrie began. A raised hand from Mikhail cut her off.

"If Emilia asks," he said to her. "You overpowered me. You're a lot stronger than you look."

Carrie laughed. "Thank you," she said to him. "You have no idea how much your help means to me."

"Thank me when it's over," he told her. "You'd better be careful. Emilia will kill me if anything happens to you." He rose from the chair and reached out his hand. "Let's go."

On a whim, Carrie grabbed the two birthday presents off her desk and shoved them in her purse. "Okay," she said. "I'm ready."

Mikhail quirked an eyebrow in her direction. "That's all you are taking?" he asked.

Carrie shouldered her purse. "Yes," she said. "I've got everything I need."

Carrie put her hand in his. His strong grip swallowed her delicate fingers. He took her over to her window and opened it. He sat straddling the sill. Carrie took a fearful breath. She decided that she much preferred crawling through a backyard shrub than falling through a fifth-story window. She began to reevaluate how much she trusted this guy.

"Let's go," he said, and before she could protest, he pulled her through to the other side.

Chapter Six:
Vidertref

Carrie landed with a thud on the hard cobblestone street of Hadariah's capitol. She looked up to see Mikhail had landed just as gracefully as she had. The sight of his gangly limbs splayed out on the ground made her feel less self-conscious as she picked herself up off of the ground. As she stood and tried to get her bearings, Carrie became aware of a steady thrumming that seemed to emanate from both nowhere and everywhere all at the same time. She closed her eyes and just let herself feel it course through her. She smiled as she recognized the strains of song coming from Elijah's violin.

"Mikhail!" called out a familiar voice.

Carrie looked up to see Emilia running toward them, red hair flying out behind her like a flaming banner. She noticed Carrie and stopped short.

"Emilia," Carrie said. "I made him bring me. Don't be mad at him."

"I am not mad," Emilia said. "I just pray you know what you are doing." She smiled. "I am happy to see you. It has been far too long."

Carrie pulled Emilia in for a tight hug. "I'm happy to see you, too," she said. "I missed you."

Mikhail approached the two girls as if unsure of whether or not he should break up their reunion. He cleared his throat, and Emilia turned to him.

"I should be upset," she said, narrowing her eyes at her friend. "But I am glad you have brought Carrie to us."

Mikhail put his arm around the princess. "Do you swear you are not angry with me?" he asked.

Emilia playfully shrugged him off. "Maybe," she said with a smirk. "Now we must go to the palace. The king and queen have some news for us all."

* * *

Carrie entered the throne room with Mikhail and Emilia at her side and gave a clumsy curtsy. As she rose, she saw the warm look of welcome on the faces of the royal couple. Once more, she was taken aback by how beautiful they both were. The queen was especially beautiful now, as Carrie could make out the swell of a pregnant belly under her lavender gown. The Queen smiled at Carrie and Emilia, welcoming her two guests into her home.

"Carrie," the king said. "We are honoured to have you back among us. We only wish it was under more pleasant circumstances."

"Thank you," Carrie said. "Emilia tells me there's news?"

"Yes," he replied. "We believe that the dybbuks who took your friends have taken up residence in a village five leagues from here."

Carrie's heart surged with hope. "Then what are we waiting for?" she cried. "Let's go!"

"We cannot allow you to just run off," the king told her. He raised his hand in a gesture asking for patience. "You must know all the relevant information. You cannot run into this blindly. If you do, I fear they will take you prisoner as well."

"The king is correct," Emilia said. "Tell us what you know."

"To the north of here," the queen began, "There is a small village called Muzikonstin. Until recently, it was a peaceful place. Now, the people are cruel to each other. Child has turned against parent, husband against wife, friendships have been utterly destroyed. We believe that this is the dybbuks' doing. This place was a town of artisans. Their creations were once light and beautiful. Now all they are creating is full of darkness and pain." She gestured to a small pageboy who stood to her right. He approached Carrie and held out two plates. She carefully took them in her hands. The first depicted a mother carrying a young child painted in exquisite beauty. Carrie could see the painstaking detail put into the mother's loving expression. The child lay in her arms with a look of utter contentment and trust. The colours were light and airy lending the scene an angelic and ethereal air. The person who had created this had obviously done so out of love. She passed the plate to Emilia and examined the second. It depicted a similar scene, but here, the mother looked at her screaming child with a glare of resentment and hate. Her beautiful features were twisted with cruelty. The child was writhing in her arms, its face contorted in an expression of fear and pain, mouth open, wailing. The colour palette was dark, full of shades of red. Carrie gasped as she saw a knife in the mother's hand, blade glinting wickedly.

"It's all like this?" she asked, as she passed the plate on.

The queen nodded gravely. "Yes," she said. "I can understand some artists wanting to explore other themes, take risks with their work, but an entire village producing things such as this… It is unnatural."

"I agree," Mikhail said as he handed the plates back to the pageboy. "When would you like us to leave?"

"As soon as possible," the king said. "We shall give you supplies and horses for your journey. We wish you much luck on your way. I would accompany you, but I do not wish to leave my wife so close to our child's impending birth."

"I understand," Emilia said. "We shall strive to make you proud and rescue Rebecca and Lindsay."

The king smiled at her. "My princess," he said. "We are already so proud of all you have accomplished."

The queen reached over and took his hand in hers. Her eyes were filled with warmth and pride. "This is true," she said. "Since you came to this court, you have become an invaluable part of this kingdom. You are beloved by us."

Emilia blushed, her pale skin turning crimson, and her violet eyes sought the floor. "Thank you," she whispered. "That means a lot."

"Go," said the king. "Get ready for your journey. I will come and see you off."

* * *

Clad in brown leather pants, a mossy green cotton tunic, and tall boots, Carrie stood in front of a gorgeous chocolate-coloured mare. She looked the animal in its soft dark eyes and tried to keep herself calm. She didn't hear Mikhail approach and jumped when he placed his hand on her arm.

"You do know how to ride, right?" Mikhail asked her.

"I used to take lessons at summer camp when I was younger," Carrie said. "It's been a while. I hope I remember how… Although, we mostly learned how to turn the horse around, and how to groom the horse. We never did any complicated riding."

"The king's animals are quite tame, I promise," Mikhail assured her. "If you can face down Asmodeus, I am sure you can ride this horse."

Carrie gave him a shy smile. "Thank you," she said to him. "Can you do me a small favour?"

"Anything," he said to her.

"Stop sneaking up on me," Carrie said to him.

Mikhail chuckled. "I will do my best," he promised.

Just then, Emilia joined them. She was wearing similar pants to Carrie's, but her tunic was a light brown, and she had put on a vest that was the same brown leather as her pants. She gave a small wave to Carrie and Mikhail, and handed Carrie a small dagger in a sturdy sheath. Carrie cautiously took it and examined it closely. She could see the handle was silver with a gold scroll design wrapped around it, coming to a ball at the end. She pulled it from the sheath and examined its slight curve and wickedly sharp point.

"Thank you," she said. "But what do I need this for? I'm more likely to hurt myself than anyone else with it."

"It is always best to have some form of extra protection," Emilia replied. "We may face more than dybbuks on the road."

Carrie took a deep breath. "I refuse to hurt anyone with this," she said. "I can't do it. Will I need one against a dybbuk?"

"It will not achieve much against them," Emilia said.

"Well then I see no point," Carrie said stubbornly.

"With luck," Mikhail said. "You will not have to use it. Just look like you can."

"Lindsay's the actress," Carrie said as she begrudgingly attached the knife to her belt. "I'll do my best though." She awkwardly swung herself into her saddle and watched as both Mikhail and Emilia mounted their horses as if they had been born to do it.

"We all will do our best," Emilia assured her. "Let us go retrieve our friends."

With that pronouncement, the three headed on their way to the village of Muzikonstin to stop the dybbuks and hopefully save Rebecca and Lindsay.

Chapter Seven:
Ha Derech le Muzikonstin

They had not gone too far on their journey before Carrie realized she remembered more than she thought when it came to riding horses. The mare she was on kept up a good pace without much encouragement, and she had no fears about falling off, or of the horse getting spooked. She, Emilia, and Mikhail kept up a good conversation, with her and the dybbuk princess catching up on all that had happened in their lives since Carrie had last been in Hadariah.

"So, you have a boyfriend," Carrie was saying.

"Mikhail was awful about him for a while," Emilia said with a laugh. "He teased him mercilessly."

"I had to make sure he was good enough for you Emilia," Mikhail said. "Remember the last young man you were with? The blacksmith's son? He was awful. I am so glad you finally saw the light with regards to him. I told you he was using you. He just wanted to be able to brag that he had wooed the dybbuk princess. Besides, I also have to like him as well. After all, if he is with you, he will be in my life, too. Although, I will admit, your opinion is the most important."

Carrie smiled. She could see Mikhail's point somewhat. "My friends and I are the same way," she said. "Whoever we see has to not only put up with our silliness, but appreciate it. If not, it just won't work. We have each other's backs. We can tell if someone's bad news. Boys may come and go, but best friends are forever right?"

Emilia nodded in agreement. "This is true. I would never give up years of friendship for someone I have just met, no matter how attractive they may be."

"Is this guy attractive?" Carrie asked teasingly.

"Oh yes," Emilia said, her smile widening. "Hair like the sun, eyes like emeralds, and so tall…"

"I'm taller," Mikhail said petulantly.

"Mikhail, the only people taller than you are the giants," Emilia retorted.

"What do you think about this guy?" Carrie asked Mikhail.

"Ferne is a very nice person," Mikhail said. "We get along quite well. It is clear he loves Emilia, and that is good enough for me."

"Why didn't he come with us?" Carrie asked.

"He is a scholar who cannot fight and never learned to ride horseback," Mikhail responded.

"I can't fight either," Carrie said. "You said I wouldn't have to." She felt panic begin to rise in her chest.

"I said that *hopefully* we would not have to," Emilia said. "But you have faced dybbuks before. With Ferne, I am the only one he has encountered, and as you can see, I am unlike the others. He would be completely out of his depth. I cannot take this risk with him, and so I convinced him to stay behind."

"You most certainly are unlike the others," Mikhail said with a fond smile. "As for myself, even though I was never formally trained to fight, I can hold my own if I must."

Carrie regarded them closely. She wondered if Mikhail's feelings for the princess were more than platonic. If so, she felt badly for him. She knew from a disastrous experience in high school what it was like to have feelings for someone who saw you as nothing more than a friend. It had taken days of movies with Rebecca and Lindsay and a lot of venting to her friends to get over it. Carrie reached into the pack attached to her horse's saddle and pulled out her skein of water. She took a long drink and saw Emilia and Mikhail pull their horses to an abrupt stop.

"What's going on?" Carrie asked. She immediately tensed in her saddle, all senses on high alert.

Emilia put up her hand, motioning Carrie to be quiet. Carrie could see four men standing in their way. They were big and broad, wearing dark clothes and had scraggly beards covering the lower half of their faces. One of the men took a step toward the princess. Carrie could see a nasty scar disfiguring the left side of his face. His right eye was milky white. He smiled at the trio with a cruel, thin-lipped grin, showing two rows of jagged, yellow teeth.

"You are travelling through my woods," he said in a gruff voice as he approached the group.

"These are not your woods," Emilia replied, her voice calm and cool. It was clear she would brook no argument on this fact.

"My friends and I would disagree," he said, causing one of the three men behind him to give a throaty chuckle.

"We were sent through these woods on order of the king and queen of Hadariah," Mikhail said. He had pulled himself up to his full height in his saddle making it clear that once on the ground, he would tower over all four of the men who stood before them.

"We do not recognize their authority," said the man with the scar. "We will be taking all of your possessions, or we will be taking your lives."

Carrie's palms were sweaty around the reins. She felt her mouth go dry, and knew that if she even attempted to use her knife, she would be laughed at and then killed. She saw both Emilia and Mikhail start to reach for their daggers. She swallowed hard, scrunching her eyes tightly closed. She said a quick prayer that they would all get through this in one piece.

"You will do no such thing," Emilia said in a low, threatening voice.

"Wait," Carrie said. The second the word was out of her mouth, she regretted it. She didn't know where the urge to speak had come from. And now she had everyone's eyes on her.

"The girl with odd hair speaks," the leader said. His friends laughed.

"Before you do anything rash," Carrie said. "Listen to me. Just one minute of your time. That's all I ask." She swallowed hard, daring to meet the man's eye.

The leader cocked his head and thought. "One minute," he said. "That's all you get." He crossed his arms across his thick chest and leaned against a nearby tree, affecting an air of dangerous nonchalance.

Carrie thought fast. She had no intention of fighting these people. She, Emilia, and Mikhail were outnumbered, and it would take at least three of her to make up the size of even one of these men.

"Whose side are you on?" Carrie asked, trying hard to keep any fear out of her voice.

The leader's eyes narrowed. "What do you mean?" he snarled.

"Are you on the dybbuks' side?" Carrie clarified. "Or men's?"

"Of course we are not on the side of those *things*!" he spat in anger. "How dare you ask this? We are men! Human men!"

"I can see that," Carrie quickly said. "We are passing through to the town of Muzikonstin to stop the dybbuks. If you let us through, we will stop their reign of tyranny." Out of the corner of her eye, Carrie saw Mikhail nod in agreement.

"Ha!" laughed the man. "The dybbuks' hold on this town and neighbouring lands is complete. There is no stopping them. How can such a little girl stop the dybbuks from what they are doing?"

"I don't know what you've heard," Carrie said. "I am the girl who came from another world and stopped Asmodeus. I was the one who brought the music back into this world. These little dybbuks who are causing trouble are nothing compared to the dybbuk king. If I stopped him, these ones will be a piece of cake."

She drew herself up in her saddle to make herself as tall as her diminutive height would allow. She tried to look as threatening as possible.

The four men looked at Carrie in shock. "Is this true?" asked one of the others. "Was it really you who did this?"

"It was," Emilia spoke up from Carrie's side. "I was there. I owe her my life. If you let us pass, the dybbuks will be gone from Muzikonstin and these lands. You have our word on this."

The leader looked back at his men. He considered this and nodded. "Let them pass," he ordered them. He turned back to Carrie and her friends. "You have my word," he said to them. "Nothing will harm you now on your way to the village. I swear this to you. However, if you fail, I will hunt you down myself. These dybbuks will be the least of your concerns. I do not like being made a fool."

"Agreed," Emilia said to him with a regal nod. She spurred her horse onward, and Carrie and Mikhail followed suit to complete their journey to the village ahead.

Chapter Eight:
Di Dorf

Mikhail stared at Carrie as they rode on towards the village. Carrie could feel his eyes on her and wondered what he could possibly be thinking. Finally, after what seemed like hours, she felt she had had enough of his scrutiny and turned her head to look back at him. The light was coming in through the leaves of the trees casting his face in a mottled shadow. She had trouble reading the expression on his face.

"What are you staring at?" she snapped.

Emilia looked at them, seeming to eavesdrop on their conversation.

"You are a fascinating person," Mikhail said.

Carrie's eyes narrowed. "What do you mean?"

"You seem scared and nervous a lot of the time," he said. "And yet, the manner in which you spoke to those bandits was incredible. You seemed to know just what to say. I was trembling in my saddle, terrified that I might have had to fight them. If you think you may be bad with a knife, you should see me try to wield one. My father refuses to let me chop anything in preparation for dinner. He is afraid I will cut off my fingers instead of the food. My skills in a fight are limited to how much I can tower over my opponent and how far I can swing my arms to hit someone." He gave a self-deprecating grin. "You surprised me. That is a good thing."

"Thank you?" Carrie wasn't sure if she should be flattered or not. "I just wanted to try to resolve our situation without violence."

"I agree," Mikhail said. "You handled it beautifully."

Carrie blushed. The more she got to know Mikhail, the more she could understand why Emilia was such good friends with him.

"I want to apologize once more for making you so uncomfortable before," he said awkwardly. "I did not intend to make you scared, or 'stalk' you as you said. I was just trying to help you."

"It's okay," Carrie said to him. "I forgive you. I understand what you were trying to do. I just hate being kept in the dark. Things would've been so much easier if you'd only come to me and let me know what was going on."

"I know that now," Mikhail replied. "I feel badly that I caused anyone any distress."

"It was my fault," Emilia broke in. "I told him it may be best if he concealed his presence. I thought he may have problems fitting in with your society. If he remained in the background of things, you might be able to continue living your life in peace."

"Ignorance is bliss, huh?" Carrie asked. "I don't subscribe to that theory at all. I need to know everything that's going on. Being kept out of the loop is one of my pet peeves. Especially if it concerns something so serious."

"I apologize as well," Emilia said. "I see now that you were right."

"I accept your apology," Carrie answered with a smile. She felt slightly vindicated that her companions agreed with her point of view.

The rest of the trip passed uneventfully. Carrie found Mikhail to be a pleasant conversationalist. His rapport with Emilia was reminiscent of hers with Lindsay and Rebecca, full of fondness and good-natured teasing. More than once, Carrie felt a pang of fear and sadness for her friends. She wondered how they were, if they remained unharmed. She missed them terribly and prayed she would get to them before it was too late.

* * *

The trio came to a break in the trees and slowed their horses so they could approach at a better pace. Carrie could feel the familiar tingling on the back of her neck. While she had been at home, it had been bearable; here, it felt as if her skin were on fire.

Emilia noticed her friend's discomfort and asked what was wrong.

"I seem to be able to sense magic," Carrie said. "Adom noticed this too when I first met him. But here, it's too much."

Emilia looked at Mikhail. "Can you do something?" she asked.

Mikhail dismounted his horse and walked over to Carrie. He reached up to her. "Give me your hand," he said.

Carrie placed her hand in his and watched as he murmured something to himself. She strained to hear the words.

"*Leygn aroyf baryerz, haltn ir zikher. Suf di tsores, shtum vos iz dort.*"

She let out a sigh of relief when the pain receded to something much more manageable.

"Are you a wizard or something?" Carrie asked curiously as she gave Mikhail a smile of gratitude.

"No," Mikhail said. "Everyone in my village had to learn ways of protecting themselves due to the fact that we live so close to Asmodeus' home. Everyone has the capacity for great magic. It is just a matter of channeling your desires into something greater. For instance, I had the desire to help you."

"So those words were more like a prayer than a spell," Carrie observed.

"You could say that," Mikhail said. "I take it from your reaction that it worked."

"Yes," Carrie said. "Thank you." She looked down and saw they were still holding hands. She turned beet red and hoped he did not notice. She carefully took her hand out of his. "How am I able to do this? Sense magic?" she asked.

"Some people possess a sensitivity," Emilia answered. "In Hadariah, it goes largely unnoticed since we are surrounded by magic all our lives."

"But I'm not used to it…so sometimes I can find it overwhelming," Carrie said, understanding dawning on her.

"Precisely," Emilia said with a smile.

"Why didn't it bother me before?"

"I believe it was because most people were in hiding," Emilia said. "All were fearful of my father, and very little was occurring. There was not much for you to sense since the land was slowly dying around us."

Carrie nodded. She regarded the thinning tree line before them. "How much further?"

"We are there," Emilia said. "Just through this last line of trees is the edge of the village."

Mikhail remounted his horse. "Then let us go," he said. "The sooner we get there, the sooner we can eat."

Emilia laughed. "Always thinking of your stomach, Mikhail," she said to him. "Does your father never feed you at home?"

"You know me, Emilia," he said. "Always hungry. There is just so much of me to feed."

"And yet," Emilia retorted, "you are still skin and bone. I despise that about you."

"So do I," Mikhail said. "Too thin. I look like a scarecrow."

"I think you look pretty good," Carrie blurted out. She felt a hot blush creep up into her cheeks.

"Thank you," Mikhail replied.

Carrie looked at him out of the corner of her eye, praying that he didn't see how red she had turned. She meant what she said. Here, in his own world, with the sun on his face, and a wide grin in her direction, she found him quite attractive. He seemed at ease here, his long limbs imbued with a grace that had been missing when she had first met him. He was not handsome by any stretch of the imagination, but Carrie liked that about him. He certainly had character. His touch was gentle, his eyes were warm, and Carrie found herself wondering if his hair was as soft as it appeared. She shook her head as if to rid it of these thoughts. She could not let herself get distracted by a boy. Not now. Especially not one who may have feelings for his best friend. She was already embroiled in a complicated situation. She had to focus on saving her friends. When she had them back, then she could look to see if Mikhail was someone to pursue.

They passed through the last row of trees, and Carrie got her first view of Muzikonstin. The sun was just beginning to set, and Carrie could see the rows of small stone houses on either side of a cobblestone street. Their thatch roofs seemed to glow in the light of the setting sun. The rooms inside of their windows were all dark.

"Where is everybody?" Carrie asked. "This doesn't feel right."

"I agree," Emilia said. "Let us ride into the town square. It is just up ahead."

They continued on. Carrie could see that the flower boxes on the windows of the houses were all dead. What gardens there were seemed unkempt; weeds were growing and choking the flowers that remained. Up ahead, she could see the square, dominated by a large fountain. Where once it must have had beautiful flowering shrubs growing around it, the garden was filled with dead, broken branches. Around it, Carrie could see empty bottles littering the ground. In front of the shops lining the square, stone benches were occupied by people. Each one sat glaring at the trio on horseback.

"Why are they just sitting there?" Carrie quietly asked.

"I do not know," Mikhail answered. "It does not feel natural."

Emilia pulled her horse to a stop and dismounted. She walked over to the nearest person, still holding her horse's reins. "Pardon me," she said. "Where may we house our animals?"

The woman turned her face to the princess. "Nowhere," she hissed. "Leave town."

"We have no intention of doing so," Emilia told her. "We wish the use of a stable and a warm meal."

"You will find no hospitality here," the woman snarled in response.

"I am sure someone will see fit to give us aid," Emilia haughtily replied. "Surely there are still righteous people among you."

The woman stiffly rose and gave them a slow, cruel smile. "You presume incorrectly. We are all the same. I know who you are, Princess. It was folly for you to come. You shall soon see that when our leader finds you."

Carrie's heart beat wildly in her chest. Had they come all this way only to ride into a trap? A sudden clattering noise broke the tension in the square, and all turned to find its source, but found nothing. Carrie looked back to see the woman had vanished.

A young child came running out from a nearby store. "Visitors!" he cried. "Are you here to help us?"

"Possibly," Emilia told him. "Can you show us to the nearest stable where we can water and brush our horses?"

"Follow me," the young boy said, gesturing.

As they walked through town, Carrie started talking with the boy trying to find out what had been happening.

"What's your name?" she asked.

"Pinchas," he answered. He looked up at Carrie with big brown eyes and a wide gap-toothed smile. "I am so happy you've come. I know you will fix things."

Carrie resisted the urge to ruffle his shaggy brown hair. He looked to be no more than five years old. "Where are your parents?" she asked him.

Pinchas frowned. "All our parents are sitting out in the square or making really scary pictures and statues," he answered. "I don't like it. The art gives me nightmares now. Sometimes the grownups get up and fight. They argue over everything. We all hide when that happens."

"All?" Carrie asked.

"Us children do not like the yelling," Pinchas said, a forlorn look on his face.

"How many of you are there?" Carrie asked him.

"There are two in the stables," Pinchas said. "Maybe more with the cakes. More in the place my papa goes to be with his friends."

"Okay," Carrie said. "No one's been hurt have they?"

Pinchas looked down at the ground and shuffled his feet. "I think my friend's mama got hurt. But she seems okay again."

"No kids have been hurt?" Carrie asked him.

"No goats," Pinchas answered. He looked at Carrie with a confused look on his face. He poked at the gap with his tongue where he was missing a tooth.

"Goats?" Carrie asked. She was as confused as he looked.

Mikhail, who had been listening to their conversation, gave a small chuckle. "Carrie means 'children,'" he clarified. "Where she comes from, they sometimes call children 'kids.'"

"Then what do they call baby goats?" Pinchas asked.

"Also kids," Carrie answered.

"That makes no sense!" Pinchas exclaimed with a laugh. "Where you come from is funny."

"Yes, it is," Carrie said with a smile. "Now, are all you children okay?"

Pinchas nodded. "Yes," he said. He stopped walking. "Here we are," he said gesturing to the large wooden doors of the stables.

"Thank you," Emilia said. She stepped forward and pulled the doors open.

They walked their horses into the stable, greeted by the smell of hay and horse. Pinchas gave a low whistle, and they were greeted by two more small children.

"These are my friends," Pinchas told them. "This is Yosef," he said gesturing to a small boy with big blue eyes and round cheeks. "And this is Chaya," he said.

A tiny girl with strawberry blonde hair and big green eyes shyly approached Emilia. "I like your hair," she whispered.

Emilia dropped down to her knees. "Thank you," she said with a smile.

Yosef walked up to Mikhail. "You're a giant," he said with wide eyes. "Can I pet your horse?"

Mikhail laughed. "Of course."

"Thank you," Yosef said to him, practically flinging himself at the animal petting its flank. "I like your horse."

"He likes you as well," Mikhail said as the horse nuzzled the small boy.

"Tell us what's happened here," Carrie told the children. She watched as Emilia and Mikhail put the horses into stalls, and they all settled in among the hay, each pulling a child into their lap.

Carrie sat cuddling Pinchas as he settled in, holding onto her. Chaya sat with Emilia idly winding the princess' long red hair around her fingers, seeming to marvel at the colour. Yosef sat in Mikhail's lap, hitting him with his tiny fists as if trying to prove to the tall young man just how strong he was.

"The grownups stopped making pretty things one day," Yosef said. "Now it all looks scary and angry. They yell at each other. Sometimes they hit each other. All the flowers are gone." He turned a mournful eye on Mikhail. "My mama used to get mad if I picked all her flowers, but when she took all of them away it was okay. That's not fair!"

"No," Mikhail said. "That is most certainly not fair."

"Did all of this occur at once?" Emilia asked. "Or did this happen over a long time?"

"I think they all got sick quickly," Chaya quietly answered. "One day my mama was happy. The next, she was always mad at me." She frowned and dropped Emilia's hair. She began picking at the dark blue fabric of her dress. "Can you really make it all better?"

"We are here to try," Emilia assured her with a hug.

Soon after, Mikhail ventured outside with Yosef as his guide. They quickly returned with a basket laden with buns, sweets, and muffins. It was clear to Carrie that they had raided the bakery, and she was thrilled. Despite the stale nature of the food, she was famished.

Around a mouthful of stale muffin, Carrie inquired after a plan. "What exactly are we going to do?" she mumbled.

Emilia looked a little disgusted with her lack of manners. Pinchas giggled from his spot in Carrie's lap.

"We need to ascertain who is in charge," Emilia replied. "Once we know who the dybbuk leader is, we can find a way to make them leave this place."

Carrie nearly choked on her muffin. She gave a few hoarse coughs before Mikhail offered her some water. "Thank you," she said to him. She looked at Emilia. "I understand that we need to help these people, but don't forget, we also have to get Rebecca and Lindsay back."

Emilia blinked a few times, "I have not forgotten that at all, Carrie," she said. "I am sorry if I made you think so."

Carrie nodded. "I'm sorry I snapped at you," she admitted. "I'm just worried about my friends."

Pinchas took Carrie's hand in his. "Did the people out there take your friends away?" he asked.

"We think so," Carrie said. "But we're getting them back."

Pinchas smiled. "Good."

Carrie could see that night had fallen through some small windows in the stable. She, Emilia, and Mikhail put the children to sleep in the piles of hay and covered them with blankets.

"I think we should go outside and speak with what adults we can," Mikhail said.

"I agree," Emilia told him. "Let us go now while the children are safe and asleep."

Carrie unconsciously touched the knife at her belt, as if reassuring herself of its presence. "Let's go," she said. She thought back to the woman in the square. Once again, she felt the fear they were walking into a trap, but could see no other way to fix what was happening to the town.

Together, the three of them went out into the night air in search of a dybbuk.

Chapter Nine:
Ha Dybbuk

The silence was eerie. Carrie could feel the presence of countless dybbuks all around her, and she knew without a doubt that they longed to do her harm. She clutched at the knife's handle at her side. Part of her had to laugh at the fact that she had not wanted it at all at first, yet now she was immensely grateful for its protective presence. Its weight reassured her, although she knew she would be awful at actually wielding it in a fight.

She, Emilia, and Mikhail walked back through the town square. It was now empty. All the men and women who had been sitting on the stone benches were gone. Somehow, this made Carrie even more nervous than their silent staring had earlier.

"Where do you think everybody went?" Carrie asked.

"I am not sure," Emilia responded.

"I have a very bad feeling about this," Carrie said.

"As do I," Emilia replied.

Mikhail motioned with his hand to get their attention. "Look," he said pointing to the building in front of them. "There is a light on in the tavern."

Emilia nodded to him. "Then that is where we shall go," she said and led the way to the tavern's door.

Carrie felt a strong sense of trepidation as they approached the tavern. From the light in the window, she could see a hanging sign. Carrie could make out the words "The Musician's Muse" as well as a beautifully rendered ivory violin. She took a deep breath as she followed her friends inside. The air within the tavern was smoky, and everything was covered in a thin layer of grime. It looked like a place that, until very recently, had been lovingly cared for. It was full of people. All were in the same unkempt state as those they had passed earlier that day. Each one was obsessively bent over a piece of paper or pottery. Some were working with clay. From what Carrie could see of the art, it was all a grotesque perversion of the warm portrait that the king and queen had shown her. One woman with the same wide eyes as Chaya was manically sculpting a man writhing in agony. Another was painting a village burning to the ground, its residents fleeing in terror. Everywhere Carrie turned, horrific images of murder, violence, and sadness assaulted her vision.

Mikhail let the door shut with a bang behind him. At the sound, all of the men and women abruptly stopped their work to stare menacingly at the intruders. Emilia stepped forward, her back ramrod-straight, exuding confidence and power.

"I wish to speak with the one in charge," she said.

A small man with mousy brown hair and a sharp pointed nose darted forward. "My princess," he sneered. "I am the one to whom you must speak."

"What is your purpose with this town?" Emilia demanded. "I am horrified by what I see here. You must leave these people and this place at once."

"We are quite comfortable here," he answered. "Your father is gone, and we no longer recognize your family's authority over us. We will not leave." His eyes kept darting from place to place as he spoke. His fingers twitched with nervous energy. He smiled at Emilia as if daring her to challenge him further.

The air around the pair seemed to crackle with tension and power. Carrie could see Emilia's fiery hair wave, though there was no breeze blowing through the tavern. The space around her seemed to glow.

"I think you will," Emilia coolly said. "Furthermore, you will tell us what you have done with the humans known as Lindsay and Rebecca."

"We have done nothing," the dybbuk said.

"You're lying," Carrie spoke up before she could stop herself. She found everyone's eyes on her.

"How dare you call me a liar," The dybbuk snarled. He shifted towards her. The air around him seemed alive with heat and full of malice.

"I will call you whatever I want," Carrie retorted. "We were told you were the dybbuks who took my friends."

A sickening smile spread across the dybbuk's features. "You are the human who defeated our king," he said.

"She is," Mikhail said. He moved to step between Carrie and the dybbuk.

Carrie stepped out of his way. "I did," she agreed. "And now, I endorse Princess Emilia's right to power. You tell us where my friends are, and you leave this village."

"Or what?" the dybbuk asked. "You destroy me as you destroyed Asmodeus? This I refuse to allow to happen." He moved his hand. A strong invisible force threw Carrie roughly to the ground. She landed heavily on the hard floor, giving out a cry of pain.

Picking herself up carefully, Carrie watched as Emilia's eyes narrowed. The princess seemed to grow taller as she drew a deep breath. A strong wind picked up inside the tavern.

Mikhail ran to Carrie's side, and the pair huddled on the floor as shards of broken pottery and glass flew through the air as if caught in an invisible tornado. The rat-faced man struggled to stay upright. Emilia's hands rose with the wind. The princess' face was dark with anger.

"Emilia," Carrie called. "Don't hurt him!"

Emilia turned to Carrie. "Give me one good reason why," she coldly said.

"The man whose body that is did nothing wrong," Carrie pleaded. "Once the dybbuk leaves him, he doesn't deserve the pain of injuries or worse."

Emilia looked contrite. "You are right," she said. She turned to the dybbuk. "You are lucky my friend is a greater person than I."

"I, however, am no person at all," the dybbuk said. He cackled with mirth and, using his power, flung Emilia into the bar. The glasses lining the wooden surface shattered on impact, covering the princess as she slowly sank to the floor. He stepped menacingly toward the fallen girl, a twisted smile on his face.

Mikhail rose to step between them as a sick feeling rose in Carrie's stomach. This was all too much like what happened when she and her friends had fought Asmodeus. She would not lose anyone else like she had lost Adom.

Acting purely on instinct, Carrie rose and pulled the knife from its sheath. "Maybe I'm not such a good person. Maybe I will destroy you after all," she said, pointing her weapon in his direction. "I dare you to give me a reason to use this." In that moment, she honestly felt that she could utilize her weapon if it meant preventing the loss of another friend.

The dybbuk's eyes narrowed dangerously. "Where did you get that knife?" he asked. He took a step forward. The look on his face promised more violence.

"It was gifted to her by me," Emilia answered in a voice laced with pain.

"You would give a human a dybbuk relic like this?" He seemed outraged.

Carrie looked sharply at the princess. Why hadn't she told her of the knife's importance? She felt angry and betrayed. Once more, things that seemed important were being kept from her. She turned back to the dybbuk.

"If you are so honest," she said to him. "Tell me why this knife is so important."

"It was Asmodeus' personal weapon," the dybbuk answered. "It was forged by a great witch, and he used it for preparing his most potent potions."

"Does it have powers?" Carrie asked.

"None other than its ability to cut straight and never dull," the dybbuk replied.

"Is this true?" Carrie asked Emilia.

"Yes," Emilia answered.

Carrie looked with disgust at the weapon in her hand. More than anything she wanted the thing as far away from her as possible. "If I give you this knife," she said, "will you swear to take every single one of the dybbuks in this town and leave these people alone?"

"I will," the dybbuk said. "Owning this knife will make all see me as a worthy leader. You do understand this."

"And as such," Carrie said. "You will owe me. Because I made it possible. Also, you will tell me all you know about where my friends are." The dybbuk opened his mouth to protest, but Carrie pressed on. "You may not have had anything to do with what happened to them, but I don't believe for a second that you haven't heard anything."

The dybbuk glared at her. "This is true," he said. "But give me the knife first, or I will tell you nothing."

Carrie looked at Emilia. She could not read the princess' expression. She turned back to the dybbuk.

"Swear on all you hold dear that you will not double cross us," the princess said.

"I swear," the dybbuk growled.

Emilia nodded, and Carrie handed him the knife.

"The sheath too," the dybbuk said, greedily eyeing it in its place on Carrie's hip.

"After you tell me what I need to know," Carrie insisted.

The dybbuk frowned. "I have heard that the group of dybbuks you are searching for is in a small town twenty leagues north of here. They are claiming they stole two human girls from their beds in another world and spirited them back here."

"What town?" Mikhail demanded sharply.

"The town of Shkalo," the dybbuk said. "Now hand me my sheath."

Carrie handed the sheath over. "Thank you," she said sincerely. Even though she despised what was being done to these people, she was grateful to be a little closer to getting her friends back.

"You have the knife," Emilia said. "Now fulfill the rest of your part. Leave this place."

A foul wind blew through the tavern, whipping Carrie's hair around her face and pulling at her clothes. She held her breath, not wanting to breathe in the putrid stench of the dybbuks as they left their hosts and the village. When she could see again, she saw the citizens of Muzikonstin slumped over their paintings and sculptures. Others were collapsed on the floor.

"Are they…" Carrie asked, afraid.

Emilia went over to the rat faced man on the floor and examined him. "He is merely unconscious."

Mikhail let out a sigh of relief. "I feared the worst as well," he said.

"We should wait here until they wake up," Carrie said. "I think they'll have a lot of questions for us when they do."

Chapter Ten:
Tshuvot

Mikhail walked over to the bar and started looking around for some food and drink. Carrie was grateful for the distraction and took charge of finding three unoccupied chairs. She soon found a table and cleared off the surface, relishing the opportunity to destroy the grisly art the dybbuks had created. She sat down and waited for Emilia to join her. Once the princess sat down across from her, Carrie took the opportunity to get a few things off her chest.

"You know I hate it when people keep things from me," she said, arms folded across her chest. "Why didn't you tell me that knife belonged to your father?"

Emilia stared at her hands. She seemed unable to look Carrie in the eye. "I thought you would not accept it if you knew," she quietly said.

"Damn right I wouldn't!" Carrie angrily exclaimed. "Why did you even give it to me?"

"I thought it would prove useful to you," Emilia replied. "I was right in that. Just not in the way I expected. I thought you could use it for food preparation, as a source of protection, intimidation…" She trailed off and looked at Carrie apologetically. "Are you still angry with me?"

Carrie sighed. The fierce princess who had stood up to the dybbuks' leader was gone. Instead she was face to face with an insecure young woman, fear and guilt plain on her face. "I'm not mad," Carrie said. "Why didn't *you* keep it?"

"I have a knife of my own," Emilia replied. "I did not need it. I knew you would be unarmed. I asked the king to allow me to provide you with a weapon. As a gift."

"Are you upset I gave it away?" Carrie asked.

"No," Emilia said.

"That is the truth," she continued. "What you did achieved our goal. We have saved these people and have new information that may aid us in retrieving our friends. This is a wonderful thing."

Mikhail came and joined them. He carried a tray laden with meat pies and tankards of ale. Carrie took hers skeptically. She was not keen on drinking, but felt that at this moment she could use it. She took a sip and grimaced at the bitter taste.

"Does it always taste like this?" she asked. She could not understand why her friends at school were always drinking the stuff.

"Do you not have ale in your world?" Mikhail asked after a large swig of his drink.

"Yes," Carrie said. "But I don't normally drink it. It's kind of gross."

Emilia laughed. "Perhaps you would prefer wine?"

"I think I'd prefer to keep my wits about me," Carrie retorted. She pushed her drink away and began picking at her meat pie. "This is good, though. What is it?"

"I believe it is either rabbit or venison," Mikhail responded. "They were not well labeled back there."

Carrie choked a little on her mouthful of food. "I'm eating rabbit or deer?" she said. "Bambi or Thumper?"

"Do you not eat meat?" Mikhail asked. "I am sorry."

"I do," Carrie said. "I'm just not an adventurous eater. My parents call me picky."

"This is adventurous where you are from?" Mikhail said. "This is common here."

"Yeah," Carrie said. "We're usually cow and chicken people."

"Your world is odd," he said.

"Yes, it is," Carrie agreed with a smile.

"Maybe I could visit at a time when I am not distracted by dybbuks?" Mikhail said awkwardly.

Carrie could feel a blush rise in her cheeks. She hoped he could not see it. "Maybe you could," she said.

Emilia was sitting with a wide grin on her face. A groan attracted their attention, and they looked up to see the young woman with the large blue eyes blinking at them in confusion.

"What has happened?" she asked. "Who are you?"

Around her, others began to awaken. Soon, Carrie, Emilia, and Mikhail were surrounded by a mass of dazed and befuddled villagers.

"I am Emilia," the princess told the crowd. "My companions are Carrie and Mikhail. We were sent here by the king and queen of Hadariah to rid your village of the dybbuks. I can assure you all that they are gone and will not return. Your village is safe once more."

A portly man with curly brown hair emerged from the crowd, his hand extended. "I am Nathaniel," he said to them. "I am the mayor of this village. My thanks to you. It has seemed like ages since we have been able to think and move freely."

Mikhail took his offered hand and clasped it hard. "It was the very least we could do," he said.

The woman who had first seen them approached. "I am Lola," she said. "Please tell me one thing."

"If I can," Carrie said to her.

"Have you seen any of the children?" she nervously asked. "I have a small daughter. Her name is Chaya. Is she all right?" She looked around as if trying to locate her child in the crowd.

Carrie gave her a reassuring smile. "We've seen your daughter," she told Lola. "She's fine. We left her sleeping in the stable with her two friends Yosef and Pinchas."

Lola clapped her hands to her mouth with a relieved exclamation of gratitude. Nathaniel smiled gratefully.

"Yosef is my son," he said to Carrie. "Did they mention any of the other children? No one was hurt, I pray."

"They told us that all the children are safe," Carrie informed the adults. "They all took up shelter in various buildings and shops when they realized what was happening."

"Thank you," Nathaniel said. "They must have been so scared. I do not know what we would have done should something have happened to any of them. We owe you all so much. You must stay at least for a celebratory feast in your honour."

Carrie hesitated. She felt that she must move on in order to find her friends, but it felt wrong to snub the village and not accept their offer of thanks.

Emilia stepped forward once more. "We thank you for your offer," she said. "We would love to accept, but we must move on. We are trying to locate some friends of ours who have been taken by a group of dybbuks."

Nathaniel shook his head. "We understand," he said. "But surely you must rest, if only for a brief time. Stay until tomorrow evening. We will feast, and then you may leave."

Emilia turned an enquiring gaze to Carrie, who nodded. They would travel better and farther if they were well rested and fed.

"We accept," the princess said with a smile.

Chapter Eleven:
Nakht

Carrie, Emilia, and Mikhail led the way to the stables with Lola, Nathaniel, and Pinchas' parents, Helena and Jacob. Carrie opened the door and led the way inside. The children's parents quietly walked in to see the three friends still fast asleep in the hay. Lola knelt down beside her sleeping daughter and softly brushed a lock of hair off her face. Chaya stirred and slowly opened her eyes.

"Mama?" Chaya asked; her blue eyes were wide with fright.

"I'm here Chayushka," her mother gently said. "I am not going anywhere. I love you so much."

Chaya gave a shout of happiness that woke the two sleeping boys. All three children flung themselves into their parents' arms and were showered with kisses and exclamations of love.

"You did it!" Pinchas shouted to Carrie. "You really did it!"

Yosef broke free of his father's embrace and ran to Mikhail. "You are amazing!" he cried happily. He gave Mikhail a giant hug around his knees.

Lola smiled at Carrie, Emilia, and Mikhail. "You will stay with me until you must leave tomorrow," she said. "I run the town's inn. I will give you a room."

"We would love to stay with you," Emilia said. "Thank you for your hospitality."

* * *

Some time later, the three of them were making themselves comfortable in their room. Carrie loved the charm of the space, with the whitewashed walls and the wooden beams across the ceiling. The room had two large beds, and they had decided that Emilia and Carrie would share. Lola had offered them each their own room, but they had declined. They felt that they should be together, just in case the dybbuks reneged on their promise to leave. Carrie was grateful for the company, not wanting to be alone. Since her friends had disappeared, she could not remember when she had last had a fully restful night of sleep.

Mikhail dropped off as soon as his head hit the pillow and was softly snoring when Carrie joined Emilia in the large four-poster bed. She snuggled deep under the warm down comforter and was happy to find that the bed was even more comfortable than it appeared. A small part of her felt guilty that they were not leaving immediately to get to Shkalo to find Lindsay and Rebecca, but she knew it would be better to have a proper night's rest first.

Carrie turned to Emilia and wished her a good night, then rolled over and settled in to sleep.

In her dreams Carrie found herself walking through the woods, the ground a mottled green and spongy with moss and dead leaves. She watched the sunlight dance through the branches and listened to the birdsong carried on the wind. She found herself exploring the way the trees grew crookedly, weaving around each other striving to reach toward the sky. Carrie felt completely at peace, unconcerned for the first time in days. She smiled and spun around, arms outstretched. A movement through the gaps in the trees caught her eye, and Carrie stopped to look. She could see the figure was the shape and size of a person. She watched it move toward her and could see it was having trouble walking properly. It was lurching forward as if injured. Carrie called toward it and took a step forward. With unease, she saw a second figure join it. The two moved in a twisted, awkward synchronicity, as if they were a pair of zombies shambling towards their prey. Carrie felt her unease build as they came closer. She felt the urge to run, but found she could no longer move her legs. She felt as if her feet had grown roots. She was stuck fast, with no choice but to watch them come ever closer, staggering, dragging themselves forward. The figures came to a break in the trees, and Carrie breathed a sigh of relief as she saw them in the light. Lindsay and Rebecca were making their way back to their friend.

"Lindsay! Rebecca!" Carrie called out to them, her mouth stretched wide in a grin. Her smile faltered as she got no answer. She squinted, trying to see her friends better. "Lindsay? Rebecca?" Carrie still got no response.

Lindsay and Rebecca shuffled closer. Finally they were near enough for Carrie to see them properly. She stifled a gasp at what she saw. Their clothing was ripped and stained with dirt and what appeared to be dried blood. Their eyes were wide and vacant, staring straight ahead and unseeing. Their hair was matted and caked with filth. Their skin was bruised and torn, pale from lack of sun. Both looked malnourished and ill. Carrie felt tears prickle in her eyes. While she had been comfortable in bed, happy with her friends Emilia and Mikhail, Lindsay and Rebecca had been held captive and tortured.

"My friends," Carrie whispered, her voice choked with sadness and guilt. "What have they done to you? I am so sorry."

Lindsay and Rebecca were finally close enough to touch. Carrie reached out a trembling hand to take Rebecca's hand. At her touch, Rebecca snarled and grabbed Carrie's wrist tightly. Carrie let out a startled exclamation of pain. At her cry, Lindsay turned and grabbed Carrie's other arm. Both of her friends' faces were twisted in anger.

"You," Lindsay growled. "You did this. It's your fault."

"You left us to rot," Rebecca said. "You went to classes, you had dinners with your parents, you laughed and talked with Emilia. All the while, we became like this. They made us like this."

"No!" cried Carrie. "I was trying to find you! I didn't know where you were! I looked and looked. I didn't know what was happening to you. I'm so sorry!" Her eyes overflowed with tears. She tried to pull her hands away, but to no avail.

"Now it's time for you to pay," Lindsay cackled. Her eyes were wild. "Now you join us."

"Please," Carrie begged. "Don't do this. There's still time. I can save you."

Her friends' hands were digging into her skin with increasing strength. She bit her lip to keep from crying out in pain. Rebecca and Lindsay leaned in, cruel smiles on their lips. Carrie could see their teeth had been sharpened into points.

"We no longer need saving," Lindsay sneered. "You're the one who does." She opened her mouth and leaned in as if to bite her friend.

Carrie woke up screaming. Emilia and Mikhail were staring at her, concern written across their features.

"What happened?" Mikhail asked, coming to sit on the edge of the girls' bed.

"I had this terrible dream," Carrie said. She still shook with the fear and memory of it all.

"Tell us about it," Emilia said. She reached over and put her arm around Carrie's shoulder. "Maybe we can make it better for you."

Carrie took a deep breath. "I was in the woods," she started. "Everything was so beautiful and peaceful. I was happy. Then all of a sudden, I saw Rebecca and Lindsay. They looked like they'd been tortured. They'd become monsters. They accused me of ignoring the fact that they were trapped somewhere, being hurt. They said they'd make me like them. They grabbed me. I remember it hurting. Lindsay leaned in as if to bite me, or eat me, or something. I don't know. It was awful." Carrie gave a small hiccoughing sob.

Mikhail reached over to take her hand. "It's over now," he said. "We will find them. This is just your concern over your friends bleeding into your dreams. We still have time. We will save them. I promise."

"Mikhail is right," Emilia said. "We will find them and save them both. Let us go back to sleep. We all need the rest."

"Okay," Carrie said. "You're right. It's just a dream."

Mikhail leaned over and gave Carrie a quick kiss on her forehead. "Good night," he said. "Only sweet dreams now."

Carrie blushed and wished him a good night. She watched him make his way back to his bed and lie back down.

Emilia looked closely at her friend. "He seems to have taken a shine to you," she said quietly, a small smile on her face.

"He's very nice," Carrie said. "I like him."

"Between you and me," Emilia whispered. "You are the first girl in which I have seen him take an interest in a long time."

"Were you and he ever…" Carrie wasn't sure how to continue.

"Oh, good heavens no," Emilia said with a small laugh. "We are just good friends. Never was more than that. Never will be."

"Oh," Carrie answered. She felt better, yet could not explain why.

"We really should sleep," Emilia said.

"Yes," Carrie agreed. "Good night, Emilia."

"Good night, Carrie."

Carrie lay awake listening to her companions breathing in their sleep. She rolled onto her side and felt a small pain in her wrist. She pulled her arm out from under the blanket. In the moonlight from the window, Carrie could make out a hand-shaped bruise forming on her wrist.

Chapter Twelve:
Ha Mishteh

Carrie woke up the next morning and stretched out in bed. She allowed herself to rest a moment, basking in the warmth of the quilt and the morning sun. The rest of her sleep had been undisturbed and peaceful. She felt a twinge in her wrist and frowned when she saw the bruise was still there. Part of her had hoped that it had been a part of her dream as well. However, seeing it in the light of day reinforced that it was real. She saw Mikhail was lying awake in his bed, and she smiled at him. She knew she looked rumpled from sleep, as did he, but she found it made him look innocently adorable. She felt incredibly shy around him, and could not remember the last time any boy made her feel that way. She made herself wish him a good morning then slipped out of bed and headed for the wash closet in the hall to brush her teeth and get ready for the day ahead.

A short time later, Carrie, Emilia, and Mikhail were sitting together around the breakfast table in Lola's dining room. Carrie was sipping at her tea and nibbling on a piece of toast slathered with sweet apple butter. Emilia and Mikhail were debating on the best route to take to Shkalo. Emilia turned to Carrie and frowned, reaching out and tenderly taking her friend's hand, examining her wrist.

"What happened?" Emilia asked.

Carrie swallowed before answering. "I don't know," she said. "I woke up with it that way." She pursed her lips for a moment, thinking before asking a question that had been nagging at her mind. "Emilia," Carrie began. "I'm still wearing my chamtzah. Why isn't it protecting me? I mean, it seems that when my 'friends' grabbed me in my dream, it really happened. None of the dybbuks in the inn touched me last night, and unless *you* attacked me in my sleep…"

Emilia sighed. "While it does offer protection," she said. "It is not absolute. It will prevent dybbuks from taking over your body. It offers some protection from them entering your mind…. However, I am concerned that your fear for your friends' plight has rendered you far more vulnerable than your chamtzah can compensate for."

Carrie nodded. "Is this why the dybbuk last night was able to throw me around like that?" she asked.

"He would have been able to do that regardless," Emilia said. "The necklace protects you from mental and spiritual attacks. If someone were to strike at you physically, it can do nothing to prevent it."

"Thank you," Carrie said. "This is good to know."

"Just know that we are here for you," Mikhail said. "We will offer what help we can."

"Thank you, Mikhail," Carrie told him. "I appreciate that."

Mikhail's grey eyes sparkled with happiness as Carrie smiled at him. Emilia beamed at her friends, and they finished their breakfast, chatting happily.

Carrie rose to clear away her dishes when Pinchas ran into the room with a package clutched tightly in his tiny hands.

"Carrie!" he cried with a large smile on his face. "Carrie! I have presents for you!"

Carrie took the package from him. "You didn't have to do this," she said to him.

"I know," he said as he rocked back and forth in place.

Carrie smiled. Since he had his parents back, it seemed impossible for him to stay still. "What is it?" she asked him.

"You have to open it," he explained. "That's what you do with a present. You open it to see what's inside."

"Okay," Carrie said. She put the package down on the table in front of Emilia and Mikhail and began undoing the wrapping. She soon found herself holding armfuls of beautiful, soft, colourful fabric. Emilia took hold of the midnight blue, Mikhail took the kelly green, while Carrie still held the burnt orange.

"That's just the one I wanted you to keep!" Pinchas exclaimed happily to Carrie. "Shake it out! Look at it! It's clothes!"

Carrie laughed and did what she was asked. She found herself looking at a simple, yet beautiful shift dress. It had long flared sleeves and a sweetheart neckline. The fabric was wonderfully soft, reminiscent of cashmere, yet felt so much lighter. The colour was somewhere between a sunset and the flames of a bonfire. Carrie held the dress to her face, rubbing it softly against her cheek. She turned to see Emilia examining hers, a similar style, but with a square neck. Her dress was a deep, inky blue, the colour of the sky on a clear night. She thought that with Emilia's fiery hair and pale skin, it was perfect for the princess. Mikhail held a flowing tunic style shirt with matching leggings. The shirt had a deep V in the neck, held closed with a dark brown leather tie. Carrie could not wait to see the beautiful green colour on him. With his dark hair and grey eyes, she knew it would look lovely on him.

Carrie turned to Pinchas. "I love it," she said.

"I as well," Emilia told him.

"Me, too," Mikhail said.

Pinchas beamed. "They're for you to wear to the feast," he told them. "My mother made them for you."

"Tell her we send our thanks," Carrie said. "They're just lovely. She does beautiful work."

"I will," Pinchas said as he ran off.

* * *

That evening, Carrie, Emilia, and Mikhail found themselves to be the guests of honour at the village's feast. Over the course of the day, the square had been transformed into the beautiful main hub of the village that it had been before the dybbuks' arrival. The fountain had been polished until it gleamed. Water merrily poured into the basin and sparkled in the light of the bonfire that crackled nearby. The dead shrubs and flowers had been cleared and replaced by a multitude of rainbow blossoms releasing their sweet fragrance into the night air. Streamers and paper chains hung from building to building, crisscrossing the square to form a multicoloured awning of sorts that spanned the length of the main street. The benches had been cleared and replaced with many long wooden tables laden covered in mouth-watering dishes of food, each looking more appetizing than the next.

Carrie wandered through the crowd feeling resplendent in her new dress. She had swept her hair out of her face and kept it pinned back with some simple bronze combs she borrowed from Emilia. She loved how beautiful and confident the dress made her feel, and found the colour gave her a glow to her complexion. She swore she could feel Mikhail's eyes following her as she walked.

Soon, the three friends found themselves swarmed by a group of children led by Pinchas, Yosef, and Chaya. All wanted to hear stories about what life was like in the palace. Had they had any adventures on their journey to Muzikonstin? How had Carrie and her friends stopped Asmodeus? What was Carrie's world like? Can they go there, too? Carrie and her friends tried their best to answer whatever they could, all with smiles and laughter. The children were astonished as Carrie tried to explain the concept of a telephone to them, and were further amazed that she lived in a tiny room on the fifth floor of a building that did not require her to take the stairs.

Nathaniel approached the group with a smile and picked Yosef up in his arms with a big hug. "Children," the mayor said, "go find your parents and have a seat. We would like to officially start the meal."

"Yay! Food!" Pinchas cried, and took off toward one of the tables.

"Good," Mikhail said. "I am starving." He offered his arms to Emilia and Carrie, and together the three of them took seats at the mayor's urging at the head of one of the tables.

Carrie loaded up her plate with a little of everything. She did not know what most of the foods were, but wanted to try it all. She took a bite of what looked like potato paprikash, and was gratified to find it tasted very similar to the dish back home. The light peppery taste combined with the perfectly cooked potato reminded her of the way her bubbie used to cook for her family on most Friday nights. She followed this with what seemed to be a slightly spicy goulash in a tomato-based sauce. The meat was tender, and she found her knife was completely unnecessary. She also tried a pungent cabbage stew, followed by a crisp, leafy salad lightly dressed in a tart, citric dressing. She could make out subtle hints of poppy seeds and pumpkin that gave it an intriguing flavour combination. There were meat pies with a flaky, buttery crust and piles of pickles teetered on plates, with a garlicky crunch that delighted her taste buds. She turned her head to see Mikhail loading his plate for what seemed like the third time. Emilia was delicately nibbling at warm, fresh egg bread with a crumbly streusel topping. Carrie wondered how any of them would ever have enough room for dessert.

When everyone had finished at least two platefuls of food, the mayor pushed himself back from the table and raised his hands to ask for everyone's attention.

"Ladies, gentlemen," Nathaniel began, "I am certain we are all aware of why we are here tonight. If it were not for the bravery of these three young people, we would all still be under the control of the dybbuks. Carrie, Emilia, Mikhail—we owe you our lives. Know that you have our thanks and our eternal gratitude. If you ever need shelter, or aid, you will always find it in Muzikonstin."

"Thank you," Emilia said. "You have our friendship as well." The crowd cheered.

"Now," the mayor said, "before we have dessert, we dance!"

With that announcement, people all around them pulled out instruments from under their chairs. Carrie could see guitars, fiddles, accordions, clarinets, and even the odd triangle. Soon a rollicking melody was being played all around her. Carrie was looking at what had to be one of the largest klezmer bands she had ever seen. She found herself being dragged onto her feet by Mikhail and Emilia in spite of her protests. She was never a good dancer, but found it did not matter here. She was being whirled around by strangers, having lost her friends in the crowd. Circles of dancers were spinning in every which way. Some people had taken to standing on tables, clapping their hands so they could get a better view of everything that was going on. Men were spinning together, and Carrie could see Mikhail with a group of men acting as a veritable whirling dervish. Emilia danced by and grasped Carrie's hand, pulling her into the centre of a circle, and the two girls spun together, laughing and smiling.

Some time later, Carrie collapsed into a seat, gasping for breath. "I haven't danced so much since, well, ever!" she said, to a woman dancing next to her as she kicked off her shoes.

"And now…dessert!" wheezed a red-faced Nathaniel.

Carrie groaned as rows of men and women began putting tray after tray of cookies, cakes, and pies on the tables. Mikhail and Emilia ran over to Carrie, and she watched, eyes agog as Mikhail began filling a plate with thick, sticky slices of apple pie, cookies speckled with chunks of chocolate, and pastries oozing cream and jam.

"How can you still eat?" Carrie asked in shock.

"This food is fantastic!" Mikhail said around a mouthful of food. "Try some." He held out his plate to Carrie.

"All right." Carrie gave in and took a cookie from the offered plate. She took a bite and smiled as the chocolate melted on her tongue. He was right. It was fantastic. She sighed and went to get her own plate full of the sweet goodies.

The party went on well into the night. Everyone was joyous and gay. Carrie finished her dessert and joined group after group in dancing. She took breaks for mugs of thick hot chocolate topped with clotted cream. Joined Emilia by the fire and toasted biscuits on sticks, which were dipped into mugs of mulled cider.

It was well into the wee hours of the morning when she and her friends finally stumbled into bed. Carrie snuggled into the blankets, head muddled, giggling softly.

"I think I like village life much better than life in a palace," Carrie said. "It's much more fun."

"Did anybody point out to her that the cider contained alcohol?" Mikhail asked Emilia with a slight chuckle.

"I fear not," Emilia said. "Although, I must confess, I do not understand how she did not notice."

"How many mugs did she have?" Mikhail asked.

"I can hear you," Carrie sang. "And I had five mugs, and they were delicious! So warm and toasty! Do you want to sing? I want to sing."

"I think we should sleep," Emilia said. "We are departing tomorrow."

"But it's a party!" Carrie said. She sat up straight in bed and flung her arms out wide. "I think we should dance some more."

Emilia pulled her friend gently back down. "I really believe you should sleep now," she told her. "Good night Carrie."

"Night night," Carrie said. She was sleeping within seconds.

Chapter Thirteen:
Al ha Derech

Carrie awoke with a groan. She turned away from the window, scrunching her eyes tightly shut, trying desperately to ignore the rolling feeling in her stomach. Her mouth tasted as if she'd been licking sawdust. Her head was hammering with intense pain unlike anything she had felt before. She just wanted to pull the covers over her head and ignore the entire world's existence. Somehow, she managed to drag herself out of bed and lurch across the room to her clothes. She did not remember how she had gotten undressed and ready for bed. The way her mouth tasted, she was unsure of whether or not she had even brushed her teeth before falling asleep. She looked around the room to find that she was alone. Emilia and Mikhail had already gone downstairs. She gritted her teeth with embarrassment. She was sure she had made a fool of herself in front of them the night before. Forcing herself to move, Carrie slowly eased her way down the stairs to the dining room.

Carrie settled into a seat at the table, wincing at Emilia's chirpy greeting and Mikhail's hearty good morning. Mikhail pushed a plate of porridge in Carrie's direction, and she tried to push it back. Its beige colour and lumpy appearance made her stomach lurch uncomfortably. The very thought of even attempting to swallow a single spoonful of the stuff made her cringe.

"We plan on being on the road today," Mikhail told her. "You must eat."

"I can't," Carrie moaned. "It might come right back up." She shuddered at the thought of suffering through another several hours on horseback.

"Wait a moment," Emilia said, as she got up and left the table. She returned a few minutes later with a steaming mug of what looked like herbal tea. She set it in front of Carrie. "Drink this. Trust me, it will help."

Carrie looked at the liquid skeptically. She gave it a tentative sniff. She smelled nothing overtly offensive. What she did smell seemed like a cross between cinnamon and liquorice. She looked at it carefully, examining the dark brown drink, and took a small sip. When it stayed down, she drank some more. As she drank, her stomach settled, and the jack-hammering pain in her head eased.

"That's amazing," Carrie said. "Thank you. Where did you learn to make stuff like that?"

"My father was always having wild parties," Emilia said. "I learned quite early on how to help his guests the next morning."

Carrie took the bowl of porridge back from Mikhail and slowly began eating it. With the headache subsiding and her stomach feeling better, she felt she could face breakfast. Her friends were right. It would not be a good idea to travel on an empty stomach.

After breakfast, Carrie, Emilia, and Mikhail stood in the square saddling their horses and making sure they had everything they required for the journey to Shkalo. A large crowd had gathered to see the trio off on their journey. Standing at the front of the large group were Chaya, Yosef, and Pinchas with morose looks on their little faces.

"I hope you find your friends," Pinchas said. "But I wish you did not have to leave." He looked down at the ground and dejectedly kicked at the dirt with his small feet.

"I'll come back," Carrie promised as she knelt to look him in the eye. "And when I do, I'll bring Lindsay and Rebecca with me. I'm going to tell them all about you guys."

"Really?" His eyes lit up at the idea.

"Really," Carrie said as she pulled him in for a tight hug.

Chaya stepped forward holding out a package wrapped in cloth. "My mom was going to give you this," she shyly said. "But I asked if I could do it." She handed the gift to Emilia, who thanked her. "It's cheese, bread, jam, and some flasks of water for your journey. That way you will not get hungry."

Yosef stood straight and tall with both hands behind his back and a serious look on his face. "My dad said I can give you all presents on the village's half," he said in a tone full of grave importance.

"*Behalf*, Yosef," Nathaniel corrected with a smile.

"I said it, Papa," Yosef insisted with a small stamp of his foot. "Here," he said, and handed three small pouches to Mikhail, Emilia, and Carrie.

Mikhail took his and pulled out a small gold compass on a thick chain. "It is beautiful," Mikhail said. "I shall treasure it."

"This way you will not get lost on your way," Yosef said.

Emilia opened hers to find a small vial on a silver chain. Inside, she could see a clear liquid.

"It stops poison," Yosef said. "I hope you do not need it."

"As do I," Emilia said. "Thank you for your gift."

Carrie reached into her pouch and pulled out a delicate silver **dagger**. It was much smaller than the one she had given away and did not seem quite as intimidating. "Thank you," she said to Yosef.

"This is to take the place of the one you traded for saving us," Yosef said. "I want you to stay safe. We all do."

"We will do our best," Carrie promised. She hoped that would be enough.

"Know you always have a place here," Nathaniel told them. "Once again, we thank you for all you have done for us. Stay safe on your journey. May you find your friends in good health and in good time."

"Thank you," Carrie, Emilia, and Mikhail said in unison. The three of them climbed up onto their horses and set off. As they left the village, Carrie turned to take one last look. She saw that the children had broken away from their parents and stood waving. She raised her hand and waved a small goodbye to them. She gave them a small smile, hoping that she would be able to keep her promise to Pinchas and bring her missing friends to meet them soon.

* * *

"How long is the trip to Shkalo?" Carrie asked when they were a short distance away from Muzikonstin.

"At the pace we are going," Mikhail answered, "assuming we stop for meals, we should be there by late afternoon tomorrow." He turned to the two girls. "I do plan on stopping for the night. It would not do to face whatever is going on in that town exhausted from our journey."

"I agree," Emilia said. "Such a plan is prudent. How and where were you thinking?"

"I picked up some tents and blankets while you and Carrie were packing up this morning," Mikhail said. "This way, we can stop whenever we feel we must."

"I'm good at camping," Carrie said. "I usually pitch the tents for my parents and friends whenever we go." She was pleased to be able to contribute in some meaningful way.

"Excellent," Mikhail said.

"I can't think that the tents here can be too different from what we have at home," Carrie added thoughtfully.

"I have never camped," Emilia said. "But I do not feel this shall pose too much of a problem."

"What's there to know?" Carrie said. "You just sleep in a tent instead of an inn or hotel, and cook your food over a fire outdoors."

"This sounds delightful," Emilia said. "I shall have to tell Ferne we should try it for fun when we get back."

"You should," Carrie said. "It's so nice to get away from city life and just be surrounded by nature. I love it."

They rode on in companionable silence. Carrie could see that they were definitely travelling down a well-worn horse path through the trees. It was so different from the last time she had travelled through Hadariah. Then, the world had been cast in darkness. She and her friends had had only a vague idea of where they were headed. She had had no idea just exactly how vast the world truly was. She supposed that this had been quite naive of her.

Emilia's voice broke through her thoughts. "What?" Carrie asked, hoping the princess would repeat herself. She'd been so caught up in her own musings that she missed the question.

"I was asking you what you were thinking of," Emilia said. "You seemed so very lost in thought. I was curious."

Carrie smiled. "I'm sorry… I was just thinking how different this trip through your world is than the last time I was here. It's a completely new experience to go from place to place in the day, with two people who are familiar with the way. However, I really need to visit when I'm not in danger. Right?"

Emilia laughed. "Yes, you really must."

The group travelled on, laughing and talking as if they had known each other for years. The events of the past few days had brought them much closer than they had thought possible. Carrie already felt that they were an integral part of the 'pack' that previously had been her, Lindsay, and Rebecca. She knew that her two best friends had already accepted the princess, and she knew with an equal certainty that Mikhail would be just as readily accepted as Emilia had been. They stopped for a simple lunch of bread and cheese under the shade of a spreading fruit tree, whose apples were a welcome addition to their repast, and soon continued on their way. Carrie watched the light begin to dim through the leaves, and knew they would soon be stopping for the night.

Mikhail pointed out a small clearing in the trees. "That looks like a good spot," he said. "If we stop now, we can pitch the tents while it is still light enough to see, and we can gather wood for a fire."

"I agree," Carrie said. "I'm getting a bit tired. It would be nice to stop."

They pulled their horses to a stop, and Carrie climbed out of her saddle. Muscles she didn't remember she had protested. Her thighs ached, as well as her back. She stretched and let out a small groan. She hoped a good night's sleep would help. She, Emilia, and Mikhail removed their horses' saddles and brushed them down before tying them to a small tree. Carrie set to work pitching the three small tents Mikhail had gotten them, and Mikhail went to collect firewood. Emilia started going through the food they had been given to prepare a meal suitable for dinner.

Carrie stepped back and admired her handiwork. She was glad she'd been right that the tents couldn't be too different than those back home. It hadn't been too difficult to sort out the poles, pegs, and canvases in order to set up three perfectly sturdy little tents. She then sorted out the blankets and pillows, evenly distributing them between the tents so that each person would have a reasonably comfortable place to sleep. She was happy she could be useful. So far, everything she had accomplished on this trip had been a fluke. She felt that the bandits on the road to Muzikonstin had just been her acting on instinct. The dybbuk had acquiesced to her, not because she knew what she was doing, but because she had had something he had wanted. Mikhail and Emilia were both experienced travellers in this world; Mikhail was a farmer and knew his way around animals and tools, while Emilia had the diplomatic training befitting a princess. While Carrie enjoyed their company and saw them both as friends, sometimes around them she felt a little out of her depth.

She went back to the packs and began looking through them to find anything else that may be useful to them that night. Stuffed in the bottom of Mikhail's pack was a small, leather-bound book. She flipped through it to see if it had information on the dybbuks, or directions to Shkalo, and was shocked to find that it contained none of these things. It was a small book of neatly handwritten poetry. Carrie could not help herself as she read through the small volume, trying hard not to laugh as she read some of the lines toward the back of the book:

Eyes like the ocean,
Wide, all seeing,
Body lithe and graceful
Wondrous being.

Emilia came skipping back into the clearing with a small basket brimming with berries and chestnuts. Carrie dropped the book as if burned. She quickly picked it up and stuffed it back in the pack.

"I thought we could have the berries as a dessert," Emilia said. "The nuts would be quite delicious roasted in the fire logs."

"Sounds great," Carrie said.

Emilia put the basket down and took a look around the clearing. "You did a fabulous job with the tents," she told Carrie. "Everything looks good."

"Thank you," Carrie said. She saw Mikhail return and waved.

Mikhail approached and set to work clearing the ground in the centre of the small circle of tents Carrie had created. She went and joined him as Emilia began pulling their food out to prepare dinner. Carrie and Mikhail soon cleared the small circle of all grass, leaves, and other plants. Carrie had trouble looking him in the eye as they worked. Mikhail built a small circle of stones, and he and Carrie built a teepee like structure of some of the larger sticks he had brought. Carrie pushed some of the smaller ones into the centre as kindling and watched in fascination as Mikhail found a piece of flint and set to work lighting the kindling. He kept trying to meet Carrie's gaze, and she steadfastly refused to look at him. He put the flint down with a sigh.

"Have I done anything to upset you?" he asked her.

"No," Carrie quickly answered. She felt her face grow hot and knew she was blushing horribly.

"Then why will you not look at me?" he asked.

"I read your journal," Carrie blurted out. Seeing the look of embarrassment on his face, she hastily continued speaking. "I'm so sorry. I thought that it might be directions, or information on the dybbuks, or something useful. I wasn't expecting poetry. I know it was private. I'm so sorry."

"Oh," Mikhail said slowly. He looked everywhere but directly at Carrie. "What did you think of it?"

Carrie did not know what to say. "Well..." she began.

"It is awful," he said. "I know. I am not that good a poet. I have no aspirations of becoming a bard, or anything of the kind. It is just something I like to do."

"I think it's nice that you like to write," Carrie said. "It's like me with my painting."

"But I saw your work on your walls," Mikhail said. "It was quite good!"

"Thank you. I liked your use of rhyming?" she said. Her uncertainty made it sound like a question.

Mikhail laughed. "Thank you," he told her with a smile. "I appreciate it."

"Mikhail?" Carrie asked.

"Mm-hmm?" Mikhail said, picking up the flint again and focusing on his work.

"Do you and your father live alone on your farm?" she said to him.

"Yes, we do," Mikhail answered. "It's just the two of us."

"How do the two of you take care of your large orchard?" Carrie asked him. Now that she had the chance, she wanted to understand more about Mikhail's life.

The Song of Vengeance

"Do you have people from the village help you at harvest time?"

"No," Mikhail said. "We have the *shretelech*. They come every year and aid us in our work. We give them gifts of food, of drink, and they have our respect."

"I don't think I've heard this word before," Carrie said. "What are they?"

"They are small creatures who dwell in the trees," Mikhail said. "They are one with nature, and resemble humans, but they are smaller in stature, with small points to their ears."

"Oh," Carrie said. "So they're like elves."

"I am unfamiliar with that term," Mikhail said. "But they may have a different name in your world."

"They don't exist in our world," Carrie said to him. "But it's pretty awesome they do here. What else is there that I don't know about?"

Mikhail than began to regale her with stories about the mischievous *kapelyushniklech*, who love horses, the scary *gilgl* who refuse to accept their death, talking animals and trees, witches and giants, towns full of fools, and the trouble-making *lantekh* who live under bridges going after travellers.

Soon, they had a small fire going, and Emilia joined them with three pillows that she had taken from the tents. They each took one and set them down as seats.

The three of them sat around the fire toasting sandwiches of bread and salty, aged cheese, watching as the cheese melted into the holes in the toast. The chestnuts merrily cracked and popped as they roasted in the embers, filling the clearing with a smoky, homey scent. Carrie was reminded of a time when she was twelve years old. Her mother had taken her on a trip to Paris for a family wedding in February. The weather had been cold and damp, but what she remembered so clearly was the street vendors selling paper cones full of roasted chestnuts fresh from their large metal drums. They were in such a large number; it seemed the whole city was full of the woodsy smell. The smell of it in the forest seemed incongruous to Carrie, since she associated it so strongly to that trip all those years ago.

Carrie took a bite of her sandwich, her teeth tearing through the crusty bread, tasting the salty aged cheddar melted perfectly over the top. She popped some of the fresh berries in her mouth, the combination of raspberry and blueberry tart and sweet in her mouth. She watched as Mikhail used a stick to swipe some of the chestnuts from the embers of the fire and pry them open with his knife. He blew on them and popped the flesh into his mouth, grinning as he savoured their taste. Carrie followed suit and let out a small groan of pleasure at the nut's woody flavour. She felt the skin break against her teeth and tasted the pulpy flesh. She felt she could eat all the nuts that sat in the fire, and still have room for more.

"They are good, are they not?" Emilia asked with a smile. Carrie merely nodded her response, mouth too full to say anything.

Carrie swallowed. "I keep forgetting how good and fresh everything tastes here," she said. "I swear I can seriously get fat if I stay."

Emilia laughed. "With all the exercise we are getting, I do not believe that is possible," she said.

"I feel that many are far too focused on looks," Mikhail said. "If you are healthy and happy, that is truly beautiful."

"Easy for you to say," Carrie said. "You're a stick!"

Mikhail laughed. "I wish I wasn't sometimes."

"I like you this way," Emilia said. "I think I might find it odd if you were larger."

"Thank you," Mikhail said to the princess.

"I like you, too," Carrie chimed in with a smile.

"And I, you," Mikhail said. "I like how small you are. I think this helped the children of the village feel less intimidated by us. They almost saw you as a peer."

Carrie put on an affronted pout. "I should be insulted by that!" she said. "My whole life I've been teased about my height. Now you're doing it, too?"

"I apologize," Mikhail said, smiling. "What can I do to show you how sorry I am?"

Carrie mulled it over. "You can give me the last chestnut," she said.

"Gladly, milady," Mikhail said with a regal bow of his head.

Carrie popped the shelled nut into her mouth and gave Mikhail a forgiving smile. "I accept your apology," she said. As she chewed, Carrie thought hard about the whole situation she and her friends found themselves in. Something about it was bothering her. "Emilia," she said slowly.

"Yes?"

"When your father ruled the dybbuks," she began, "did they often pull stuff like this?"

"What do you mean?" Emilia asked her.

"Like, take over towns and make the people create horrible things. Like, kidnap girls. Like, whatever it is they're doing to Shkalo." Carrie paused and looked inquiringly at her friend. "Emilia, what kind of king was Asmodeus?" she asked.

"As far as a ruler of the dybbuks could be considered fair, he was a fair king," Emilia replied. "And to answer your question: No. When my father ruled, things like this did not occur. When he wanted control of a town, he would send people out to take it in crafty ways, but never to the scale you see now. He never kidnapped anyone from your world, to my knowledge anyway, and he kept a tight reign on his subjects."

Carrie looked lost in thought. "So," she said, "aside from the whole destroy the world thing, it's almost as if we would be better off if he were still around controlling things."

Mikhail looked at Emilia with concern in his eyes. The princess seemed upset by the turn the conversation had taken. Carrie noticed what had happened and quickly changed the subject.

"Has Mikhail shown you how well he can build a fire?" she asked. She realized how ridiculous this segue sounded and pretended her sandwich was the most interesting thing she had ever seen, examining it intently in her hands.

"We should be getting to bed," Emilia said once the last of the food had been eaten. "We have the rest of our journey ahead of us tomorrow."

"Agreed," Mikhail answered.

Carrie, Emilia, and Mikhail stood and took their pillows. Saying their goodnights, they entered their tents. Carrie felt her skin crawl and quickly took a furtive look around the campsite. She saw nothing, but said a quick prayer that her sleep would be undisturbed.

Chapter Fourteen:
Iberrashn Gast

Carrie slept. She had closed her tent as tightly as the wooden toggles on the opening flap allowed. She had no idea what she was trying to keep out, only, that she felt safer doing this. She had wrapped herself tightly in blankets, and piled her pillows around her, trying to make a cocoon of warmth and safety. She had briefly considered asking one of the others if they would bunk with her, but rejected the idea. She had not wanted to concern them needlessly. It had taken a while, but eventually the crackling of the dying fire and the soft breathing she heard in the neighbouring tents lulled her to sleep.

In the early morning hours, before the sun had risen, a small scratching sound pulled Carrie out of her sleep. She sat up, blankets falling around her. It sounded as if a small animal was trying to find its way into her tent. She sat holding her breath as she saw the canvas of the tent bulge in at the opening, thankful that the toggles were holding tight. The scratching grew in intensity, and Carrie let out a small squeak of fright as the first toggle gave way. A small black nose poked through, followed by a red fur snout, and the rest of a head. Carrie's eyes widened in shock as Adom walked into the tent. She pinched herself and was surprised that she actually felt the pain. She was as awake as she could possibly be.

"How are you here?" she whispered. "You're dead." She winced at how cold her comment sounded, and instantly wished she could take it back.

Adom turned in place and sat down on the floor of the tent. He cocked his head to the side and gazed at Carrie. "I have come to warn you, Carrie," he said. "Do not go to Shkalo."

"Are you a ghost?" Carrie asked. "I don't understand what's happening." Carrie drew her arms around her knees to ward off the chill that seemed to permeate the air in the tent.

"Carrie," Adom said, concern written in his deep brown eyes. "It is unimportant as to how I am here. Please just heed my warning. Do not go to Shkalo. There is nothing but pain for you there."

"Adom," Carrie said. "I have to go. Don't you understand? I need to go to find Lindsay and Rebecca. I can't just forget about them and leave them. I have to save them, and Shkalo is the only clue I have telling me where they are."

"I do understand," Adom said sadly. "Is there nothing I can do or say to convince you not to go there?"

"No," Carrie said defiantly. "Please tell me what's wrong with that place. What's so awful that I can't go there?" She leaned forward, every bit of her begging for answers.

"For everyone it will be different," Adom answered. "I cannot say exactly what form it will take for you. Just heed my warning: Trust not what you see with your eyes. They will deceive you."

"How?" Carrie asked. "I don't understand." She reached out for Adom, but he backed away from her hands.

"I am sorry," he said. "I cannot say more. My time here is done. Please Carrie, heed my words. Use your heart. Trust in yourself."

Carrie watched as he turned and left the tent. She crawled over to the entrance and pulled it open to look for him in the clearing, but he was nowhere to be found. The fox had disappeared. She crawled back into the tent to find that the warmth had returned, and she snuggled back down under her blankets; yet in spite of her best efforts, sleep eluded her. She lay wide awake, going over the conversation repeatedly in her mind. Had that really been him? Had Adom really come to her with a warning? She thought so; however, a small nagging doubt whispered through her thoughts: What if that had been a dybbuk? She had seen them shape-shift before. What if this was all a trick, designed to make her give up on her quest?

* * *

Carrie was unsure of how much time had passed until she finally heard Emilia and Mikhail stir. She pulled herself out of her tent and immediately set to work dismantling the structure. She systematically put all the posts in a pile and began folding the canvas. She was so lost in her work she did not notice Emilia approach until the girl put her hand on Carrie's shoulder, causing her to jump in fright and drop her armful of fabric.

Emilia apologized. "I did not mean to startle you." She peered closely at Carrie's face. "Are you all right? Come," she said as she took Carrie by the hand. "Let us sit and have some breakfast before we finish packing up."

Carrie allowed herself to be led toward the fire-pit, and sat down. Emilia put a portion of bread, cheese, and a couple of apples on a plate and handed it to Carrie. Mikhail was sitting and grinding roasted coffee beans with a mortar and pestle to be boiled with some water. Carrie sat, ate, and watched him work. Emilia seemed to be waiting for something, and when Carrie finished eating, the princess asked her what was wrong.

"Adom visited me this morning," Carrie said. "At least, I think it was him. He didn't act like he wanted to hurt me, or anything. He seemed like himself, but sadder. He warned me about going to Shkalo. He said what was there would hurt me, and I should stay away."

"Were you dreaming?" Mikhail asked. "Did this happen in your sleep?"

"No," Carrie answered firmly. She shook her head to emphasize her point. "He was real! I know it sounds crazy, but I pinched myself to see if I was asleep and I wasn't. After he left, I tried to go to sleep and couldn't. This all happened when I was wide awake. I swear it! The weird thing was, he didn't act like a ghost. He was solid. He was really there. He actually had to undo the toggles of my tent to come in and talk to me."

"We believe you," Emilia said softly. "Could this be a dybbuk? Could this have been a trick?"

Mikhail looked at Carrie earnestly, his large grey eyes looking deep into her blue-green ones. "When you said we were still going to go to Shkalo, what did Adom do?" he asked. "That is what you told him, correct?"

"Yes," Carrie answered. "I did say that. When I told him, he told me that when I got there, I should not trust my eyes, but my heart. It sounded like whatever's going on there may try to play tricks on us. He seemed genuinely concerned for me."

Mikhail nodded. "I do not think what you saw last night was a dybbuk."

"I agree with Mikhail," Emilia said. "It sounds like you met an *ibbur*. If he was speaking with sincerity, we need to proceed with caution."

"A what?" Carrie's brow knitted together in confusion.

"An ibbur is the soul of a righteous being, who still has much to accomplish," Mikhail explained. "It can possess someone living, with consent, in order to pass on a message, or fulfill an unfinished task."

Carrie's eyes welled up with tears. "So," she said. "You're saying that Adom possessed another fox to come give me a message. He was trying to protect me."

"Yes," Emilia said. She put her arm around Carrie. "He did not know you long, but it seems he cared enough about you to still want to help you, even now when it is difficult for him." She turned to Mikhail. "We need to heed his warning. We must anticipate grave troubles in Shkalo."

Mikhail nodded in agreement as he handed out tin mugs of freshly brewed coffee. Carrie accepted hers gratefully, taking small sips of its steaming bitterness.

"When we are finished eating," Emilia said. "We must pack and leave quickly. The sooner we get to Shkalo, the sooner we can get Lindsay and Rebecca back and be done with this business."

Chapter Fifteen:
Chaverim

Carrie, Emilia, and Mikhail rode onwards to Shkalo. The mood was tense as they all pondered Adom's warning.

Sunlight lit the way, giving everything a false sense of happiness and hope. The flowers were in full bloom underfoot, and the fruits in the trees all seemed to mock her with their cheerful colours. Carrie could not shake the sinking feeling that where they were headed was devoid of any hope at all. This thought also infected everything she thought with regard to Lindsay and Rebecca. If this town that is full of innocents is being treated so horribly, then what were the dybbuks doing to two young women who had helped destroy their king? Carrie shuddered at the macabre turn of thoughts. She prayed that her imagination was coming up with worse things than reality was supplying for her absent friends.

"What are you thinking about?" Mikhail asked, breaking the silence.

"I was wondering what we'll find when we get to Shkalo," Carrie answered. She left out her fear for her friends, wanting to keep some thoughts private.

"It is more than that. I'm sure you are worried for your friends. I know I would be. But you cannot think about that right now," Mikhail said; a sorrowful look on his face. "It will destroy you. You must have hope for them. We will save them."

"You can't know that," Carrie said gritting her teeth in frustration. "You just can't. It's not *possible* to know that. And even if we do save them…" She paused and tried to compose herself. "What are the dybbuks doing to them right now? Where are they keeping them? I highly doubt it's in some palace, or beach resort. I remember how Emilia was when we found her in Asmodeus' dungeon cell. She was nearly dead. She was cold, sick, starving…" She turned and saw Emilia watching her intently. "Emilia," Carrie said. "That was your own father doing that to you. What would a group of dybbuks do to a couple of strangers who defeated their king?"

Emilia looked away. It was clear to Carrie that the princess did not want to answer her question. That look told her all she needed to know. She felt tears well up in her eyes. She tried hard to stop them from overflowing.

"Let us hold on to what hope we have," Emilia finally said. "I believe the dybbuk we encountered in Muzikonstin would have given us some indication had he known our friends had been killed. I got no such feeling from him. Furthermore, the dybbuks who had taken them would surely be crowing their ultimate victory over the girls who stopped their king, and we would have heard something about it." She gave Carrie a small, encouraging smile. "As to how they are being held, no, I do not believe it is anywhere pleasant. Nor do I believe it to be anywhere comfortable. But the sooner we get to them, the sooner they can be back with us, back with people who care for them."

"Worrying for them is not going to speed their release," Mikhail said. "It will only make you more tense. But know that we do worry. We are praying for them. I promise you this."

"Thank you," Carrie said. "I can't help it. They're my friends. How can I not worry?"

"I know," Emilia replied. "It is impossible not to have so many concerns for them."

A small brown shape caught Carrie's eye as it flitted through the branches above. She followed its progress as they moved. Through the gaps in the foliage above, Carrie could see a small brown bird. She could not be certain, but she had a strange feeling it was following them as they travelled. She thought about pointing it out to Mikhail and Emilia, but did not know how to do it without making the bird aware that she knew. She figured that if the bird was following them, there was a chance it was an animal like Adom or the nightingale she had met the last time she had been in Hadariah. That bird had been on her side, trying to warn her about the false princess, Asmodeus, travelling with them disguised as his daughter. Carrie decided that if this bird was an ally, it would make itself known eventually, and so kept silent, merely tracking its progress with her eyes.

Two hours later, a twinge in her lower back prompted Carrie to halt her horse. She called out to Emilia and Mikhail, and they stopped riding looking back at her in concern.

"Guys," she said. "My back's a little sore. Can we stop for a short break? I think I should stretch my legs a bit and try to walk it off."

"I think we can do that," Mikhail said. "We are making excellent time. We will definitely reach Shkalo before nightfall at this rate."

The three of them tied their horses and gave them water. Carrie stretched herself out as best she could and began walking a little, always mindful to keep

Emilia and Mikhail in eyesight. The little bird followed her progress as she went. Carrie gestured at it with a little wave and watched, mildly surprised as it flew down to a low branch at eye level with her. She smiled upon discovering it was a nightingale as she had suspected.

"Hello," Carrie said to it.

The nightingale cocked its head to the side and peered at her with tiny, bright black eyes. "Hello," it chirped back.

"Why were you following us?" Carrie asked.

"I do not know if you recognize me," the bird said. "I have met you before. You were with the princess then, as you are now. Why?"

"The princess is my friend," Carrie said. "She is a friend of the king and queen of Hadariah. She lives with them now. Didn't you know that?"

"I had heard rumours of this," said the bird. "But as I do not live near the palace, I had no way of verifying this. If you say it is true, I will take your word for it. Why are you heading toward Shkalo? I heard that boy say that is where you were going."

"We are going to find my friends," Carrie said. "You remember seeing them with me, right? They were taken by a group of dybbuks. We were told that's where they are. What do you know about what's happening in Shkalo?"

"I am unsure as to the exact nature of the troubles there," the nightingale said, hopping nervously from foot to foot.

A branch cracked as someone approached where they were. The bird flew up to a higher branch, and Carrie whirled to face whoever was coming.

"Mikhail," Carrie said, seeing him approach. She looked up to the bird. "It's okay," she said. "He's a friend. You can trust him."

The bird flew back down. "Hello," he said to Mikhail.

"How do you know Carrie?" Mikhail asked.

"We met the last time I was here," Carrie answered for the bird.

"I tried to warn her," the nightingale said. "She seemed unaware of the origin of certain members of her party."

"He's talking about Emilia," Carrie said. "He doesn't trust her."

"Many do not," Emilia said.

Carrie marvelled at the princess' ability to move so silently. She had not heard her approach at all. She turned and saw the little bird puff out his feathers in fright.

"I am sorry," Emilia said to the bird. "I understand that my father did many awful things to many people, but I am not my father. I have been working for good. I have been trying with all that I am to correct the wrongs he did to so many. Please accept my apology for him."

"If you are indeed beloved by the king and queen, that is enough for me," the bird said with a small bow of his head. "I was telling Carrie what I know about Shkalo. Unfortunately, it is not much. The animals of the forest now avoid going through the town. It leaves all with a bad feeling. No one goes there anymore, and no one leaves. From what I hear, all who dwell there are terrified every day, and at night, rumour has it that it is a place filled with death. That is exactly as it is put: 'filled with death.' I do not know what that means. I am sorry I cannot help you more, but that is all I know."

"Thank you," Carrie said. "That is a big help. At least it gives us some idea of what's going on. I appreciate it." She gestured to her friends. "We all appreciate it."

The bird nodded at them and flew off into the forest. Carrie turned to Mikhail and Emilia with a bit of a helpless shrug.

"I saw him following us," she said. "I didn't want to scare him off. Can you make sense of what he said? What does that mean?"

"You did well to be cautious with him," Mikhail said. "It is better to have this information. You might not have gotten it if you had called out to him. The birds are notoriously skittish creatures. But they do have the ear for gossip. Unfortunately, I am as in the dark as you. I have never heard of a town described like this." He turned to Emilia, as if to ask her opinion.

"I do not know," she said. "But I can tell you, it leaves me filled with unease. I do not like this. But we must travel on. Whatever is wrong with Shkalo, we must face it for our friends' sake."

Chapter Sixteen:
Shkalo

The town of Shkalo looked as if it had once been a thriving place, full of life and joy. Every building had the appearance of being lovingly cared for once upon a time. Yet now, everywhere they turned in the light of the setting sun, Carrie could see it all covered with a light patina of dust and neglect. The windows of all the building were dull and dirty. The cobblestone streets were in disrepair. The gardens were alive, yet overgrown, and weeds were threatening to choke the flowers that grew there. Carrie looked around, trying to find any signs of human life. She heard no birdsong, no horses other than their own. No dogs barked, and no children played. Even in Muzikonstin, as they rode through the village, they had heard chirping birds, noises from the stables.

A door slammed, startling Carrie and causing her to jump in her saddle. She looked toward the noise and saw a pale, nervous looking young woman dressed all in black exiting the nearby inn. Carrie gestured to Emilia and Mikhail, drawing their attention to the woman, and they rode toward the inn. The woman in black saw them approach and looked at them with an expression of absolute fear.

"Hello," Carrie said. "We've been travelling for awhile and are looking for a place to stay. Are there any rooms available?"

"Please just go," the woman said in a hushed voice. "You cannot stay here. You must leave this place." She nervously looked from side to side as if she were afraid of being seen speaking to these travellers.

Mikhail dismounted his horse. "We came from Muzikonstin," he said. "We know there is something wrong here. We can help. Just tell us what is going on here."

The woman shook her head, eyes filled with tears. "No one can help," she said. "Please, I asked you already. Leave this place." She looked around, seeing the sun continuing to set, her eyes widened further with fright. "You cannot be here at night. You must leave."

Emilia approached the pair. "We cannot keep travelling," she said. "We can set right whatever is happening. Please let us help."

The woman shook her head. "No. This is impossible."

"Do you know who we are?" Emilia asked. "I am Emilia, the daughter of the king of the dybbuks. This is my friend Mikhail, and this is Carrie. She is the one who defeated Asmodeus and saved Hadariah when the strings of the violin were stolen by my father. Give us a chance to help. If anyone can help you, I believe we can."

"Is this true?" the woman asked. "Is this who you are?" She held her hand to her heart, as if daring herself to hope.

"Yes," Emilia said. "This is the truth."

"I can give you a room and some food," the woman said. "But you must promise not to go outside tonight. The night is not safe."

"We can do that," Emilia assured her.

"I am Mina," the woman said. "This is my inn. You can stay here tonight. We will speak more tomorrow."

Carrie, Emilia, and Mikhail gathered their belongings and followed Mina inside. They were shown to three comfortable rooms, and put their bags on the single beds. Mina went into each one and nervously drew the curtains tightly closed, as if afraid that someone outside would see she had guests. She then led them back downstairs to a large kitchen where she seated them at the table and served them a thick beef stew that had been cooking in a large cast iron pot in the hearth.

Carrie began eating, dunking some biscuits into the stew and washing it down with apple cider that Mina provided. All the while, they tried to question Mina on what was going on in the town. She remained tight-lipped about the situation, steadfastly refusing to answer any of their questions. As they spoke, they could see how tired and worn their hostess looked. Her brown eyes were red rimmed from crying and ringed with dark circles, almost looking bruised in the firelight. Her black hair was hastily pulled back in a bun, as if she simply did not care about how it looked. Her hands shook as she brought them their meals. Her clothes hung on her as if she had lost a lot of weight in a hurry, and over the rounded collar of her black dress, they could see her collarbone jutting out in sharp relief.

All through the meal, Mina barely ate. Once she was certain that her guests had all they needed, she sat and picked at her food, merely pushing it around her bowl with her fork. She made a show of taking small bites, but Carrie could see that only a tiny amount passed her lips. She refused to answer any of their questions. Carrie found it rather odd. She claimed she wanted their help, yet would not tell them what was happening in the town. She seemed far more concerned that they be shut tight in their rooms by nightfall. Carrie, Emilia, and Mikhail finished their dinner and nodded at each other. They excused themselves from the kitchen, and Carrie could see Mina's relief that they were going up to bed. Once up the stairs, they gathered in Carrie's room, and pulled the curtains back to look out over the courtyard. The sun had set, and they could see a gathering mist begin to cover the town.

"She wants our help," Carrie said. "But she won't tell us why."

"Something has her scared," Mikhail said. "I suspect the whole town is afraid."

"But of what?" Carrie asked. She kept going over the nightingale's words about how this was a town 'filled with death.'

"Look," Emilia said. She pointed out at the mist. A section of it had broken off and was gathering at the inn's door. Carrie watched in amazement as it began to take human form. A young woman, looking no more than sixteen years old, walked to the entrance. Carrie could see that she resembled Mina in complexion and stature. She walked with an expressionless look on her pale face. Carrie heard the knock as the figure reached the door, and heard Mina answer it downstairs. She looked at her friends, mind made up, and went to the door of her room. She eased it open, carefully, trying hard not to make any noise, and crept slowly into the hallway. She crept forward, aware that Emilia and Mikhail were following close behind. Soon, she could hear the voices of the two women downstairs.

"Beth, please." Carrie recognized the voice of Mina. "You cannot keep coming back. Please leave me be." The young woman sounded wracked with grief.

"I am here because you want me here," Beth replied. "You have not let go. I will keep coming to you until you do. I have more things I need."

"I have done everything you asked," Mina said. "Please no more."

"It was your fault, what happened to me," Beth insisted. "You owe me."

"What do you want?" Mina asked. Her voice sounded hollow and weak.

"There are three people here," Beth said. "We know all about them. You must give them to us. They will be ours. They have done things, horrible things. Tomorrow night, you will turn them over."

"What will you do to them?" Mina asked.

"That is none of your concern," Beth said.

"I need to know," Mina insisted.

"They will be punished," Beth answered. "We have already punished others like them, who are guilty of the same crimes."

"I have until tomorrow?" Mina asked.

"Tomorrow night," Beth confirmed.

Carrie heard the front door click closed, and she, Emilia, and Mikhail exchanged looks as they listened to the young woman downstairs sob softly in the kitchen. Wordlessly, the three friends made an agreement to remain silent, all knowing that it would not be a good idea to let their hostess know they had heard all. Morning would soon come, and they would talk then. In the meantime, they needed to know what was happening. They found their way to a back staircase and slowly went downstairs and out a back way. They carefully walked outside and into the mist, cautiously exploring the town.

The mist was about waist high. Carrie experimentally waved her hand through it, trying to get a feel for what it was. She felt clammy all over, and got chills running up and down her spine. She turned to her two friends, and saw that they felt the same. Everything about this felt wrong. Carrie shuddered and kept walking on, with Emilia and Mikhail close behind. Movement up ahead made Carrie pause. She saw a small boy coming toward them, his pale face and blond hair contrasting sharply with the darkness around them. Carrie saw his dark eyes, almost black holes in his face, peering out at them; his mouth was contorted into a cruel grin. He could not have been more than seven years old, yet he walked toward them with the cocky assurance of someone several times his age.

"What is that?" Carrie asked. "Is that a dybbuk?"

"That is," Emilia began, "of sorts, a restless spirit that cannot find peace, controlled by other dybbuks, forced to continue on as one."

"What do you want?" Emilia asked, coming forward.

"You will be ours soon enough," the boy said.

"Who are you?" she asked him.

"We are the dead," the boy said. "We have come to settle our debts."

"We know no one in this town," Emilia told him, her hands on her hips. "We therefore have no debts here."

"But you owe those who are our masters," the boy replied. "It is to them you will be given, and when you are delivered, we will have peace."

Carrie shivered. There was something about this boy that was not quite right. She remembered what Adom had told her. Was he an illusion? Was he a false spirit? She did not know what to think.

"What if we could help you without sacrificing ourselves?" Carrie asked.

"There must always be a sacrifice," the boy said. "You will make yours tomorrow."

The boy turned and began walking away, dissolving into the mist. Carrie turned to her friends, a helpless look on her face. "We must help these people. Somehow."

"We will," Emilia replied. Carrie could see that the princess was not confident in this assurance.

Chapter Seventeen:
Boker

Morning dawned, a damp grey day that reflected the mood of the people in the inn. Carrie woke up and winced as her bare feet touched the cold wood floor of her room. She looked gratefully at the steaming basin of hot water that Mina had thoughtfully put in her room for her to wash up with, and splashed it on her face before she brushed her teeth and went downstairs. She had layered her tunic with a thick woollen shawl in an attempt to keep away the chill that seemed to permeate the air around her. She found Emilia and Mikhail already at the table, and saw that they looked as cold as she felt. Somehow, the sight made her feel better, knowing she was not alone in her discomfort. Carrie sat and nodded a greeting to her friends, pulling a hot mug of coffee toward her before adding sugar and a splash of milk. She took a sip and felt the warmth spread through her. She sat back waiting for the caffeine to kick in. Mina entered the room and put a serving dish filled with hard-boiled eggs on the table.

"I trust you slept well," Mina said to them. She seemed hesitant to look any of them in the eye.

"The bed was very comfortable," Carrie said. "Thank you."

"Come and sit with us," Emilia said, gesturing to a chair.

"Thank you," Mina said, taking a seat and picking an egg from the dish. She began systematically peeling the shell.

"Mina," Mikhail said. "Who is Beth?"

Mina looked up sharply. "Where did you hear that name?" she demanded.

"We heard you speaking with her last night," Carrie said, neglecting to mention how they had been eavesdropping.

Mina looked intently at the egg in her hands. They were trembling terribly. "Beth is my sister," she whispered. "If you heard us, then you know what she wants from me."

"Yes," Carrie said. "We do."

"I need her to go away," Mina said with tears in her eyes. "She needs to stop coming back here."

Carrie thought about the boy they had met behind the inn. "I'm sorry to have to ask," she began. "Is Beth dead?"

Mina nodded. "She died last year," she whispered. "It was my fault."

"What happened?" Carrie asked. She thought about what she had just asked and winced. "You don't have to answer that," she added hastily, not wanting to seem insensitive.

"She was working in the inn with me," Mina said. "We inherited it after our parents died. I always hated getting the water from the well for the rooms and the cooking, but I had to do it. I was taller and stronger than she. One night, I was running behind. She was being so difficult, not wanting to help with anything. I yelled at her. Called her ungrateful, and said that I was doing everything, and she was a nuisance and I resented her for it. I told her to go get the water. I said she had to. She never came back." Mina looked up at them with a tear stained face. "She must have lost hold of the bucket and reached too far to get it back. She fell in. We did not find her until the next day. I thought she had gotten angry with me and run off. She did that sometimes. Now she comes by every night. She says I owe her for her death. She blames me, and she's right to do so."

Emilia put her hand on top of Mina's. "You could not have predicted such a thing," the princess told her. "You should not blame yourself. That thing that comes by every night and hurts you, that is not your sister. It is a form of dybbuk. Please trust me on this. I know my own kind."

Mina looked startled. "You…" she said. "You are a dybbuk?"

"I told you who my father was," Emilia said.

"Yes, but you are so nice," Mina said. "And Beth…"

"Beth is being used against you," Emilia said. "Did you love your sister?"

"Of course I did," Mina answered.

"What is happening is that the spirits of your dead are being used against you," Emilia explained. "They are being manipulated and forced to hurt the ones they love, and the ones that love them. They have been turned against you by a dybbuk, and when that happened, they became dybbuks as well. It is cruel and must be stopped." Emilia smiled kindly. "Please know that when we stop them, your sister and those like her will once again be at peace."

"Can you stop them?" Mina asked. For the first time since they had met her, a hopeful look crossed her face. It was only for an instant, but Carrie was certain it was there.

"I think we can," Carrie chimed in. "We helped the village of Muzikonstin. We stopped Asmodeus. Why shouldn't we be able to help you?"

A genuine smile appeared on Mina's face. Seeing it made Carrie realize Mina was far younger than she had originally thought.

"Thank you," Mina said. "May I go and tell others about your presence? If we can help, I am sure they will want to be a part of ending this horrible nightmare."

"Of course," Emilia said.

"The more the merrier," Carrie added.

Mina ran off heading out into the town leaving Carrie, Emilia, and Mikhail sitting at the table eating their breakfast.

"Do you think we can trust her?" Mikhail asked once they were sure Mina was gone.

"I do not know," Emilia said.

"I think she does mean well," Carrie said. "Look at it from her perspective: She's being harassed every night by the spirit of her dead sister. Just look at her. She's a total mess. I highly doubt she's had a good night's sleep since any of this started. I know that if this were happening to me, I would be falling apart. We're the only hope she's got. Why wouldn't she want us to stop all this?"

"You have a point," Mikhail said. "But I have some concerns."

"Like what?"

"It seems clear from our conversation with the boy last night, that it is known we are here," Mikhail said. "We must anticipate that others were given the same offer as Mina. We must think that there may be those in this town who wish to turn us over to the dybbuks."

"You're right," Carrie replied.

"What do you suggest we do?" Emilia asked.

"I don't know," Mikhail said. "We must think about this."

Carrie sat, lost in thought, as Mikhail and Emilia discussed different strategies for dealing with the problem plaguing the town. She could not help thinking that they were at a distinct disadvantage. The dybbuks had been there quite a while longer and had the townsfolk terrified, exhausted, and emotionally in turmoil. They needed some way to get the upper hand. They had Emilia, a dybbuk, and the daughter of their former king, and Carrie had her necklace, so she was probably safe from possession, if not outright harm. They also had Mikhail...who unfortunately seemed like a bit of a liability, unless...

Carrie jumped up as an idea hit her. "Wait one second! I'll be right back." She raced up to her room and quickly rummaged through her pack, grinning as she procured a small box. She ran back to the kitchen where she was greeted by a confused-looking Emilia and Mikhail.

"I was thinking that we might have a bit of a problem tonight," she said. "I have my necklace, so the dybbuks can't possess me, or do anything too horrible in that way, and Emilia *is* a dybbuk, so I doubt they can take her over."

"Right," Emilia said. "I am safe in that regard."

"But Mikhail's just, well, Mikhail," Carrie finished.

"Thank you for pointing out my ordinary nature," Mikhail said drily, a sardonic smile on his face.

"Well," Carrie pressed on. "I'm going to fix that."

"How?" Mikhail asked.

"With this," Carrie said as she presented him with the box. "I know it's a little girly. It was going to be Rebecca's birthday present, but I think she'd understand me giving it to you."

Mikhail opened the box and took out the silver filigree chamtzah. He smiled. "Thank you," he said. "This is an excellent idea. It is much better that we all be protected in some way." He put it around his neck and tucked it under his tunic, giving Carrie a warm look of gratitude.

"I have a second one as well," Carrie said. "I just wasn't sure if dybbuks were able to wear them. I don't know, maybe like vampires and crosses or something."

Emilia looked confused. "What?" she said. "Never mind. I do not require one, but I am glad that you have thought of a way to protect Mikhail."

"So what do we do?" Carrie asked. "Have you come up with a way to save the town and get Lindsay and Rebecca back?"

"Well," Mikhail said, "it is possible that we may be able to talk to these restless spirits and convince them to leave their loved ones alone. The trick is to differentiate between who is an actual spirit, and who is the dybbuk in charge keeping them here. This may be easier said than done."

"If they are at all like the boy we saw last night," Carrie said pensively, "I don't think they will want to sit down and talk."

"This is true," Emilia agreed.

Mikhail sat drumming his fingers nervously against the table. "We cannot just go around speaking to these spirits," he said. "We do not know them. We do not know who they are, what they desire, who their loved ones are. We are in the dark. What we need is to convince the people of this town to rise up and cast them out."

"And then what?" Carrie asked. "The last one standing is the dybbuk we need to defeat to get my friends back? And besides, how can we get the townsfolk to figure out which of these spirits is fake?"

"The dybbuks are not psychic. They will not know every intimate detail of these people's lives," Mikhail said shrugging his shoulders. "Unfortunately, this is the best plan we have."

"It's the only plan we have," Carrie amended. "It's better than nothing I suppose."

A knock on the kitchen door caused all three to turn in surprise. Mina stood there nervously. They waved her in, and she came to join them at the table.

"I spoke to the mayor," she said. "I told him what was happening, about who you are, and what you said you may be able to do for us. His wife Hannah has been visiting him each night just as my sister has been coming to me. She asked him to bring you to her as Beth asked me to do. He does not like the idea of sacrificing anyone to these spirits, as I do not. He wants to have a town meeting. He is calling it for this afternoon, after the lunch hour. He wants you three to be there to address the town and tell everyone what you told me. Tell them about your missing friends, how you helped Muzikonstin and defeated Asmodeus. Maybe we can put an end to all of this." She looked up at them, her eyes beseeching, begging for some hope to cling to.

"We will be there," Emilia told her. "We will speak to your town, and we will come up with a way to help you." She gave Mina a grim smile. "There is one thing you must know, Mina," she continued. "You must all be strong. It is this strength that will help you all through this far more than anything we can do for you. We are facing some malicious spirits. As you know, my father was their king. As one of them, I am all too aware of the pain they are capable of inflicting. You will have to stay sure in your resolve. When you see Beth again tonight, remember what we told you today—that she loved you and what happened to her is not your fault. Can you do this?"

Mina nodded. "I think I can," she said quietly. "I *know* I can," she repeated in a stronger voice.

"Good," Emilia said. "Hold onto that thought with all your strength. You will surely need it."

Chapter Eighteen:
Shtot Bagegenish

The town hall was a large, imposing building made of roughly hewn grey stone. Its face was dominated by massive polished oak doors with wrought iron handles and hinges, and there was a large, round window centred above the main entrance divided into eight sections. Carrie had never seen a colder, more uninviting structure in her life. It seemed quite incongruous that such a simple-looking town would have such an ugly main place of meeting. She took a deep breath and looked to her friends. The three of them had decided to change into the outfits that Pinchas had given them for the feast in order to make the best impression on the townsfolk as possible. They held each other's hands and walked into the meeting as a united front, prepared to face whatever resistance they might find.

Standing before the town, Carrie was struck by the thought that their choice of clothing may have been a mistake. She supposed the dress of mourning worn by Mina may have been a clue as to the entire town's mental state. And now, looking out at the sea of black cloth dotted only by the occasional splash of grey in a shawl or jacket, she felt that she and her friends may have unintentionally insulted everyone in their attire of bright orange, green, and blue. She tried to keep a friendly, yet sympathetic look on her face as she listened to the mayor introduce them. She cringed inwardly as he glared at her. She had to look at him with her neck craned all the way back. Even though he was stooped with grief, his tall, nearly skeletal frame even dwarfed Mikhail. She supposed his attitude toward her was more for her attire than anything she had said or done.

"These three are here to help us," the mayor was saying. "We were told that they helped drive the dybbuk scourge out of Muzikonstin. The two women were among those responsible for saving our world when Asmodeus stole Elijah's strings. I say we listen to what they have to say. There is no harm in trying to find a way to end our plight without any sacrifice of life."

A young woman whose hair was the same pale blonde as the boy they had seen the night before jumped up from her seat. Carrie could see her face was grey with pain, her lips pale. Every inch of her seemed tense and tired. Her hands were shaking.

"What can they do?" she cried. "No one can help us. Our pain is already too great. Even if these spirits were to leave, what good would that do? What's done is done. Cannot everyone see this?"

Carrie took a step forward. "Everyone here has lost someone," she said. "My friends are missing, and it is still possible that we can get them back. Why must more people die? It doesn't have to be that way."

"Who have you lost?" the woman demanded. "Who have you ever had to watch die? What do you know of pain? My son is gone." She looked at Carrie angrily, tears in her eyes.

"I lost my bubbie," Carrie said. "And the last time I was here, I watched a good friend of mine die. His name was Adom, and he was murdered by Asmodeus. I know that isn't the same, but it is still a loss to me, and I feel it deeply."

"Has he come to you at night?" the woman cried. "Does he remind you every day that you were not there when he needed you?"

"He has come to me," Carrie said. "I have seen Adom since. However, he does not make me feel guilt about his passing. He has tried to help me." She paused. "This is what we need to say to you: think hard about your loved ones. Think hard about the good times you shared with them. How they made you feel in those good times. Hold your cherished memories close to you. Do you sincerely believe that those people, the people you remember fondly, would truly wish to cause you the pain you are feeling right now?"

Several people in the hall slowly began to shake their heads. Carrie could see many people were crying. She heard a murmur of assent rumble through the crowd.

"What my friend Carrie is saying is correct," Mikhail said, stepping forward. "What is happening is that a dybbuk is using your loved ones to cause you pain. We need to find out who that is. Which of these spirits is the dybbuk we seek? You need to speak with your night visitors. Find out if they truly are those you have lost. Know that when this is settled, your relatives and friends will finally have peace. They are being used horribly. This dybbuk is being unspeakably cruel to all involved. This must end."

Carrie turned to Emilia to see if the princess had anything to add to the proceedings. However, the girl who was usually so well spoken and persuasive was standing still and pensive, eyeing the crowd with a sad look in her eyes.

The mayor looked out over the crowd. "Is there anyone here who still believes that we should turn these outsiders over to the spirits?" he asked.

Carrie felt a distinct chill radiate through her as she realized that there might be people here who were actually willing to give her and her friends over to the dybbuks. It sickened her to think that these townsfolk had become so desperate and were so hurt that human life no longer held value in their eyes. She looked nervously at the faces in the crowd. She saw Mina, who gave her a small smile of encouragement. The mother who had argued so strongly with her looked truly sorry about what she had said. There were a few faces who still seemed hesitant to give up on their idea of turning Carrie and her friends over, yet no one spoke out over the mayor.

"If this is truly the consensus," the mayor said, "then we shall do as these three suggest."

"Okay," Carrie said decisively, "what we need is to find out who is in charge. Ask the spirits personal questions when they return tonight. If they are truly your loved ones, they will know every answer, every detail about your lives together. Furthermore, you will be able to help them. You can break the hold the dybbuk has on them. You can reason with them…because deep down, they are still your wives, husbands, parents, siblings, children, and friends. The dybbuk is none of these things. He or she will only be able to give you cursory answers. They will know the basics of your life: where you work, where you got married, were born, when your birthday is, things like that. But the truly important details, like how it felt when you proposed, the exact way you smiled when you walked down the aisle, how your child's hair smelled the first time you held him. These things will be unattainable to the dybbuk. When we have their identity, we can deal with them and make them give me back my friends and break their hold on this town."

"So when we find the leader," the mayor asked, "we come and get you in the inn and take you to the dybbuk?"

"Exactly," Mikhail said. "The three of us can hopefully outnumber and overpower them."

"Any questions?" the mayor said to the assembly.

A blonde woman in the front row raised her hand.

"Yes, Edith," the mayor said with a nod.

"Judah," Edith said to the mayor. "Once we do as you suggest, and we find this dybbuk, will the spirits be gone for good?"

"One can only hope," Mayor Judah said, a sad look coming over his thin face.

Carrie was struck by the thought that maybe some of these people did not actually want the spirits to stop visiting. Maybe they clung to the visits as a way to continue seeing their family members even though they had passed on. This seemed to her to be incredibly sad, yet she understood. The visit she had had with Adom, even though it ached to know he was dead, had given her another opportunity to speak with her friend. She would love to have that same chance with her bubbie. She reached up to touch her necklace. Even though these visits were horribly unpleasant, it was still another chance to connect with someone these people loved, and stopping them would take that chance away, probably forever.

"I am glad this will soon be over," Edith said. A look of palpable relief had spread over her haggard face. "If you can achieve this, I will be eternally grateful."

A murmur of agreement spread over the townsfolk.

"We will try our best," Carrie promised. "That is all we can do."

"Thank you," Judah said. He turned back to his people and raised his hands to get their attention. "We all know what we must do. If anyone has any questions, or need advising in what they should say, Carrie, Mikhail, and Emilia will be at Mina's inn. Meeting adjourned."

Chapter Nineteen:
Vartn Far Nakht

If there was something Carrie truly hated more than anything else, it was waiting. Knowing that something important was going to occur, with nothing to do but wait for it to come, was excruciating. She despised not being able to speed up the time to make it happen already. Sitting in Mina's kitchen waiting for night to fall was driving her crazy. A large part of her was desperate to have this all over with. An equal part of her was dreading the impending confrontation and would do absolutely anything to have it not happen at all.

Mina was doing her part to make sure that everyone was as comfortable as possible. She seemed to find the simple act of baking relaxing. She was biding her time stuffing her guests with endless pots of coffee and tea, as well as plates of hot buttered scones, biscuits, endless flavours of cookies, cakes, and pastries. Carrie watched in amazement as Mikhail seemed to have an endless appetite. She quickly lost count of how many tasty treats he was able to pack away in his stomach.

"How are you not sick?" she asked him. "Where are you finding room for all this food?"

"I only had one hard-boiled egg for breakfast," he said. "Besides, Mina is working hard making us all of this food. I do not want to seem rude by not eating it. Anyways, I am quite nervous, and I tend to eat when I am nervous."

Carrie shrugged. "Just don't throw up because you ate too much. Okay?" She reached out and took a cookie. It was still warm from the oven, and she noticed that it was similar to the oatmeal cookies she used to make at home with Rebecca and her mother when she was younger. She hoped that saving her friends would set everything right.

"Emilia," Carrie said.

"Yes?" Emilia looked at Carrie with a tired look.

"Did you sleep at all last night?" Carrie asked upon seeing the look on her friend's face.

"Very little," Emilia said. "This whole thing is quite upsetting to me."

Carrie nodded in agreement. "I wanted to ask you something," she said. "Back home, when Lindsay and Rebecca went missing, everything was made to seem as if they had never even existed. My parents forgot all about them. Their own parents forgot they'd even had daughters. If we find them, will that all go back to normal?"

Emilia frowned. "This is powerful magic," she said. "Mikhail did not mention any of this to me. If we find your friends, I am sure it will break whatever spell has been cast. We will make this a part of any deal we make with the dybbuk in charge."

Carrie instantly caught on to the fact that Emilia had said 'if' when it came to finding Lindsay and Rebecca. She said nothing, thinking that this was merely a part of Emilia's stress. She looked at the princess with a considering gaze. "What kind of deal did you have in mind?" she asked.

Emilia sighed. "I have some ideas," she said. "I ask that you both trust me. I cannot say at the present time. This will only work if the dybbuk thinks you know nothing. And so, you must know nothing of what I am thinking."

"I do not like this, Emilia," Mikhail said. "You have never kept things from me before. Please do not start now. I beg of you. Before we left, Ferne asked me to watch out for you. How can I do this if you are making plans without us?"

"Ferne should know that I can take care of myself," Emilia said with a small, sad smile. "Mikhail, when it comes to the dybbuk people, I am still their princess. That carries some weight with most of them even with my father gone. Please trust that I know what I am doing. I am planning no violence, no fight. Just let me try my plans."

"I'm with Mikhail," Carrie said. "I don't like this any more than he does. However, I do trust you. Just promise me that if things look like they're going badly, trust us as you expect us to trust you. We can help."

"I promise," Emilia said.

"That will have to do, I suppose," Mikhail said with a grim look on his face.

Mina came into the room with a hot apple pie and sat it down in front of Mikhail, who immediately placed a piece on his plate. In spite of the fact that she felt quite full, the delicious cinnamon smell made Carrie's mouth water, and she cut herself a small piece as well.

"Everything is absolutely delicious Mina," Carrie said. "Thank you so much."

"You are quite welcome," Mina said. "Edith is in the front room. She would like to speak with you. May I show her in? I did not want to interrupt you if you were discussing anything important."

"Of course," Emilia said. "Send her in. We would love to help her in any way we can."

Mina turned and left, returning shortly with Edith in tow. The slight, blonde woman stood awkwardly in front of them wringing her hands. Like everyone else they had seen in town, the lines of exhaustion seemed to be permanently etched across her face. Everything about her looked worn and drawn.

"Please, sit down," Mikhail said to her. He rose and pulled a chair away from the table, gesturing for her to take a seat.

"Thank you," she whispered. She sat and looked down at her hands.

"I heard what you had to say at the meeting," Carrie said. It seemed to her that someone had to start the conversation. Edith did not seem eager to speak, regardless of the fact that she had sought them out. "How can we help you?"

"Is it really true that you can help us?" Edith asked. She tentatively raised her eyes to look at them.

"I believe it is possible, yes," Emilia said. She reached out and took Edith's hands into her own. The blonde woman clutched at them as if they were a lifeline.

"My husband refused to go to the meeting," Edith said. "He said I was foolish. I do not believe he thinks anyone can possibly make this nightmare end. But I must know, what can I possibly ask my son to see if it really is him?"

"Is there something that only the two of you would know?" Emilia asked her. "Did the two of you have a special phrase, or song? Was there a special memory that was shared only between you and him?"

Edith sat and thought. She twisted a plain gold band around and around on her finger, a nervous habit that struck Carrie as being similar to her habit of playing with her necklace. She saw Emilia was trying to be patient with Edith, giving her time to sift through years of memories. Finally, Edith met her eyes.

"I used to put my boy to bed each night asking him, 'How much does Mommy love you?' He would say that I loved him to the moon and back. But this time...he did not know," Edith said. "I would then tell him that 'Mommy loves you to the sky and back, around the world and through the stars. That is how much your mommy loves you.' Do you think that will do?" She looked at them with tears welling up in her blue eyes.

Emilia gave Edith a sad smile. "I think that is perfect," she told her.

Edith left soon after. Carrie, Mikhail, and Emilia sat silently. Carrie distractedly sipped at a cup of tea, not even registering that it had gone cold. "Why are they being so cruel?" she asked quietly. "The sheer amount of pain being inflicted upon these people is astounding. I don't understand what they're trying to accomplish here."

"I believe that this is part of a power play," Emilia said. She looked at Carrie, her eyes alight with fire. "I believe that the loss of my father has left a void that this dybbuk wishes to fill. What is happening here is on such a scale that no one will be able to deny their power. This will enable them to step in as a new ruler. You are correct—this level of cruelty leaves me certain that we cannot allow this dybbuk to assume their desired role. They must be stopped."

"I agree," Mikhail said giving Emilia a considering look. "I will say again, that I wish you would let us in on your plan. I do not like going into this blind." He reached out and took her hand. "You have been my best, most true friend for countless years. I do trust you. I trust you with my life. You know that. This is not about trust. This is about me fearing you are about to do something rash with *your* life."

"I understand," Emilia said. She squeezed his hand tightly. "I do not believe I will be in danger. Trust in that."

Carrie looked at Emilia. The princess seemed so sure of herself. In that instant, she did trust that her friend. She would trust her with her life. However, like Mikhail, she did not trust that the outcome of her plan was one that she and Mikhail would like.

Chapter Twenty:
Imut

Carrie's legs were cramping terribly as she sat perched at the top of the stairs. She longed to be able to stand and stretch them out, but she feared being seen. Night had fallen, and she and her friends had taken up position waiting and listening for the spirit of Beth to make itself known. So far, she was late. Mina sat in the kitchen below, and from the sound of it, she was on her sixth cup of tea. Earlier that evening, they had seen the mist creep across the town, and knew that their time was coming. They had taken space at the top of the stairs where they had previously heard Mina and her sister speaking, so they would know the instant anything happened. Carrie knew they were taking a huge risk. It was still possible that someone, anyone in the town, might change their mind and attempt to just hand them over to whoever was in charge. The people who were at the town meeting had not appeared completely enthusiastic about the idea that they should turn down the deal that had been presented by the spirits.

Down below, a sudden noise made Carrie take notice. She turned, wide eyed, and waved at Emilia and Mikhail. She pointed downstairs, and they nodded. They listened as the front door open and heard the shuffling of feet.

"Beth," Mina said.

"Have you decided to turn over your guests?" Beth asked. Her voice sounded as if she were quite far away.

"No," Mina said. "I cannot do that."

"You are making a big mistake, my sister," came the cold reply. "I told you that this would free you."

"You are wrong," Mina said, a note of sadness crept into her voice. "I am already free. I know that what happened to you was not my fault. Beth, it was an accident. It was a horrible accident. I never wished such a thing on you. I did not push you into the well. I never forced you to go collect the water. You know this."

Mina sounded choked with tears. "We used to argue all the time. If you truly had not wanted to help me, you would not have gone." Mina paused. "Do you remember when we were younger? When we used to run away from home? How we would go off on our own, away from our chores, and our work? How we would be together having adventures?"

"Yes," Beth said. She sounded as if she were coming out of a trance; a note of happiness entered her voice. "I remember, my sister. I remember we would run off into the woods. We would say that we would live among the shretelech. We would stay out under the trees for hours, happily dreaming about how they would find us and make us one of them. Father would eventually find us. Oh! How we were scolded! But we would always do it, again and again. I miss those days, Mina."

"As do I," Mina said. "Sister, if you love me, do not make me put others in harm's way."

"I do not want to do this," Beth said. "I am told it is the only way I may find peace."

"Let me give you peace," Mina said. "Please, know that I hold no anger toward you. You have nothing but love in my heart. I miss you and our time together, but want nothing but happiness for you. Go and find this."

"I wish I could," Beth said.

"Then please do," Mina told her. "Go in peace."

Silence descended on the inn. Carrie let out a shaky breath. She waited, straining to hear what was happening.

"Please come down," Mina called up to them. "I have no desire to be alone right now."

Carrie stood and went quickly down the stairs. She entered the kitchen to see Mina standing with tears streaming down her pale face. She opened her arms, and Carrie drew her into a tight hug, holding the small woman until the sobs subsided. Mina pulled away, her face red and eyes swollen.

"I feared it would be worse," Mina said, "losing her twice. But it is almost a relief. Now I know that she does not blame me, at least not anymore. I also know that she is free. This is a comfort I can keep in my heart and be glad of."

Emilia nodded. "Your sister was not the dybbuk we seek," she said. "You did well. This could not have been easy for you."

"No, it most certainly was not," Mina said. She sniffed and wiped her eyes with a handkerchief she had tucked away in her sleeve. "Even so, it was worth it. I may have failed her in her final hours, but I helped my sister in the end."

"So now what do we do?" Carrie asked.

"Now we wait," Emilia said as she took a seat. She casually poured herself a cup of tea and stirred a spoon of sugar into the brown liquid.

"I cannot stand waiting," Mikhail said as he joined her. "Every part of me itches to jump up and do something. This is unbearable."

"I'm with Mikhail," Carrie added. "This sucks. I know the dybbuk is out there, and here we are having tea. But I know there is nothing we can do. We need the people here to find us the dybbuk. Otherwise we are at a distinct disadvantage."

Mina nodded and joined the small group. "I see your point," she said. "I cannot tell you how relieved I am that it was not my sister. What is your plan of action once you have ascertained the dybbuk's identity?"

"Emilia has an idea," Carrie said. "But it relies on secrecy, and even we aren't in on it. However," she continued quickly after seeing Mina's concern, "we trust her completely. I know it will turn out alright."

A knock on the door caused Carrie to jump. She looked up to see Judah enter. He looked more worn than she remembered.

"Mister Mayor," Carrie said. "Your Honour, are you alright?"

He removed his hat and helped himself to a seat. He gestured to the teapot. "May I?" he asked.

"Of course," Mina said. "I also have some biscuits if you like."

"No, thank you," he answered. "Tea is fine." He turned to Carrie with a sad smile. "I am fine. The dybbuk was not my Hannah. Nor was it the doctor's mother, my neighbour's husband, or another dozen citizens' loved ones. I have been out doing rounds, checking on people. It seemed the least I could do. We are down to six people. The night is almost over. I am certain that at this point, the dybbuk has some idea that its hold on this town is breaking." He took a sip of his tea. "They cannot possibly be in the dark that people are not acquiescing to their desire for you and yours to be turned over to them."

"You are very possibly correct," Emilia said. "This means that if we get no answers tonight, it is quite possible we can visit all six homes tomorrow and drive the dybbuk out into the open."

Judah nodded grimly. "Good," he said. "I will not allow this to continue on much longer. This is my town. These are my people. I have a responsibility to them. I offer you any help I can give."

"Thank you," Mikhail said. "This is much appreciated."

Judah turned to Mina. "Is that offer of biscuits still available?" he asked.

"Of course," Mina said with a smile. She rose to fetch them and a plate for the mayor.

Carrie noticed the mayor watching their hostess move about the kitchen, and nudged Mikhail with a small smile. He saw where she was looking and nodded.

It was clear to her that the mayor fancied the young innkeeper. Maybe when this was all over she would play matchmaker.

Mina returned with the food and placed it in front of Judah. "Here you go, Your Honour," she said.

"I have told you before to call me Judah," he said kindly.

"Yes, Judah," Mina replied, blushing prettily.

Suddenly Mina looked up sharply, eyes wide with concern.

Carrie turned to see what Mina was looking at, and saw Edith standing in the kitchen breathing heavily. A blonde man stood next to her, eyes red from crying. They were holding each other's hands tightly.

"What is it?" Carrie asked. "What's wrong?"

"Our son," Edith gasped. "I asked him my question. I said, 'How much does Mommy love you?' and all he said was, 'A lot, Mommy.' I rose to back away from him. I knew then that he was not real. He saw that I knew. My husband, Simon, came into the room, and he could tell something was wrong."

"The look on his face," Simon said, turning to Carrie, "it was all wrong. Our son would never look at anyone so cruelly. I grabbed my wife by the hand, and we ran here. Edith said you can help us. Please, help us!"

"Where was the dybbuk?" Carrie asked. "Where did you leave him?"

"I do not know," Edith said. "I believe we may have been followed. When we ran, he was sitting in the parlour of our home, but now..."

Emilia and Mikhail rose to join Carrie, and the three of them exchanged looks. It was now or never. The dybbuk would have to be faced.

"I think we should go out into the town's square," Mikhail said. "We now know we are looking for a little boy. We call for him, and he comes to us. We have the upper hand."

"If he knows we know what he is," Carrie said, "won't he turn into something else? Our plan is flawed."

Emilia frowned. "This is possible," she said. "Yet, I believe that Mikhail is right. We need to go out there strong." She turned to Carrie, "Are you ready?"

Carrie nodded. "Yes," she replied. "Let's go."

* * *

The night air was unusually still. The ground was covered in mist. Carrie stumbled a few times, unable to see where she was putting her feet. Mikhail took her by the arm, steadying her and giving her a reassuring squeeze. They walked into the square, presenting a united front to whomever may be there watching. Judah and Mina had come with them despite the trio's objections. They hung back, trying to be supportive, watching and waiting and needing to see this through to the end.

Carrie thought she heard movement and turned, trying to see where it was coming from. A small form approached. It was smaller than a child, keeping far too low to the ground, and seemed to be moving on all fours. Carrie shivered. She shut her eyes, willing this not to be happening. She heard Emilia draw a sharp breath, and knew that what she feared was true. Carrie forced her eyes back open and was faced with the horrific spectre that was Adom. But it was not the Adom she had seen in her tent a couple of nights before. This was the Adom she had held in her arms in Asmodeus' throne room. This was the Adom with singed, blackened fur, the Adom that was wounded and dying. She stifled a moan, and tried to force back her tears.

"You did this to me," Adom said to her. "This is your doing. I was at peace. I was free. Now, because of you, I am here on this night. You should have stayed away. It was bad enough you let me die. Now I cannot even find peace in death."

Carrie began to sob. "I'm sorry, Adom," she said. "I am so sorry."

Mikhail grabbed her hand. "Remember what Adom told you on his last visit," he whispered. "This is not your friend."

Carrie remembered. The little fox had told her to trust her heart, not her eyes. She shut her eyes and thought hard. Her heart knew that what Mikhail said was true. A true friend would not be saying these things. The Adom she knew had been the one who came to her offering aid and concern. He had been a true friend saving her from Asmodeus' flames. She knew she was not responsible for what had happened to him. Anger filled her heart.

"You lie," she said as she opened her eyes once more. "I did not kill my friend. Asmodeus did that. You are not Adom. You are a cruel and horrible dybbuk. How dare you use these people's loved ones against them? You disgust me."

The dybbuk laughed. "You act braver than you feel, little girl," he said. "What are you going to do to stop me? You can do nothing. I can leave this town, but I will always be able to find another. You cannot follow me around your entire life."

"Maybe not," Emilia said stepping forward. "But I can."

Carrie looked at her friend filled with concern and fear. Emilia's hands were clenched tightly at her sides as she walked toward the dybbuk.

The dybbuk's eyes narrowed. "You," he sneered. "You are a traitor to your people, one who lives among the humans with her human lover. You are going to stop me?"

"I will," Emilia said. She stood straight and tall, and took a deep breath as if steeling herself for something awful. "I claim my right as Asmodeus' true heir to rule you as my father did. You will accept my authority or suffer what consequences I deem fit."

"Emilia!" Mikhail cried, shock and pain written across his face. "What are you doing?"

"Silence, human," Emilia said. Every inch of her radiated with the power Carrie had seen in her father. She seemed a formidable presence. "Do not speak to me like this in front of my subjects."

"Your subject?" the dybbuk growled. "I do not recognize you as my leader."

Emilia stretched out her hand, and the dybbuk strained as if against an invisible force. He bowed low to the princess. "It looks as if you do," she said coldly.

The dybbuk pulled himself off of the ground, and the air around him shimmered as he shifted. Carrie could feel the magic in the air and swallowed her fear as she watched the dybbuk grow ever larger in front of her. Soon there was no child, no Adom, and she found herself looking into the eyes of Asmodeus. He smiled, a slimy cruel smile, and laughed in Emilia's face.

"You really think you can take his place?" he asked. "You are nothing. You are a weak little girl playing dress up as ruler of the dybbuks. I know many choose to follow you, but you are no pure blooded dybbuk. You ally yourself with humans, and cavort with their king and queen. You betray your heritage and your father. You have no authority over me and mine. I reject your dominion over me."

Emilia took a step forward. "You do not deserve to stand in my father's place," she spat. "You say I am nothing? You are a pathetic excuse for a dybbuk. What have you accomplished here? A whole town of people managed to throw off the yoke of your power in the span of one night. You think someone such as you can take over my father's reign? Ha! I can dismantle all of your efforts with very little exertion on my part." She smiled a cold hard smile. "Furthermore," she continued, "I wish the return of the humans known as Rebecca Campbell and Lindsay Smith. I know it was you who had them taken, and you will return them to me."

Carrie stood and watched this exchange in fascination. Part of her believed that Emilia taking over the rule of the dybbuks was a good thing, while another was filled with fear for her friend. What would such a thing mean for the princess? What would she be giving up? She turned to the dybbuk to see what he would say to the demands and watched as he morphed out of Asmodeus' form. Where the dybbuk king had stood, was now a small repulsive creature, skin mottled green, spikes growing from its back. It stood naked, yellow eyes staring angrily at the princess, mouth agape. Carrie could see rows of sharp, pointed teeth.

"I cannot return them, Princess," he said in a raspy voice.

"You will," Emilia demanded. "And once you have, you will be placed in the dungeon in my father's castle. My castle," she amended.

"I cannot return them, Princess," the dybbuk repeated.

Emilia stepped forward and took a firm grasp of the dybbuk's ear. She pulled him close. "You will return my friends," she hissed at him.

"I cannot," the dybbuk whimpered.

"Give me one good reason why," she challenged.

"They are beyond my reach," he said.

Emilia threw the dybbuk to the ground. "Where are they?" she asked. Her fists were clenched at her sides. She seemed to vibrate with anger.

"Gone," the dybbuk said.

"Gone where?" Carrie asked, running up to where they stood.

The dybbuk turned away, refusing to answer.

"Gone where?" Emilia said in a low and dangerous voice.

"They are trapped in your father's mirror," the dybbuk said. "I had them brought from their world, and when I took them to your father's castle, they were pulled through his mirror. Everyone knows that when something goes in, it is impossible to bring them back out. I became scared. I did not want such a thing to happen to me, so I had one of my followers take the mirror far away. I did not see him again. I know not what became of him."

Emilia snapped her fingers at the dybbuk, and he vanished. Carrie stared in disbelief at the spot where he had been standing.

"He recognizes my authority," Emilia said. "He is now in a cell in my father's dungeon. I believe he was telling us the truth."

"What does this mean?" Carrie asked. She could feel panic rising in her. "Where are my friends? How do we get them back now?"

"We need to find my father's mirror," Emilia said. She looked defeated. "Unfortunately, what the dybbuk said is true. No one knows how to get anything out from within it."

"How do we find it?" Carrie said. "Do you have a plan?"

"No," Emilia said.

"No," Carrie repeated. "How can that be? You *always* have a plan."

"This time I do not," Emilia said to her friend. She looked exhausted.

Mikhail stepped toward them. "I have an idea," he said. "My father and I have always been kind to the shretelech. They are masters at locating things. We can go to the woods and ask if they may be willing to aid us in our search."

"Do you think they will?" Carrie asked hopefully.

"I think they might," Mikhail said. He turned to Emilia with concern in his eyes. "Do you realize what you did here tonight?" he asked her.

"I do," she said.

"Why did you do this?" he asked.

"It is what was best for this world," she answered. Her eyes were full of tears. "As the dybbuk said in Muzikonstin, there must always be sacrifice. I made mine tonight. I chose what I felt was better for everyone. Should I have left things as they were? Should I have left it that the dybbuks continue to torment the humans? Or that someone like myself steps in and takes control?"

"My whole life, you have always said that you never wanted power like your father's," Mikhail said. "You hated what power did to you. You never liked having to use it. Are you sure you want to do this?"

"No," Emilia sighed. "But I do not see what choice I have."

Mikhail nodded. "I understand what you are saying," he said. "Know that I will always be your friend, and I will always be around to keep you grounded. I am sure Ferne will as well."

"Me, too," Carrie said. "I'll also help you redecorate the castle. Make it more your style."

Emilia laughed. "I am glad I have people like you by my side."

"We always will be," Mikhail assured her.

Mina stepped forward from where she and Judah had been standing by. "Come back to the inn," she said. "We all need our rest from the events of this night. Tomorrow you can continue to search for your friends. I do not recommend going to the woods in the dark."

"Thank you," Emilia said. "We gratefully accept your hospitality."

"Thank *you*," Judah told her. "You have done us a great service. If we can do anything to help you in return, you only need to ask."

"We will," Mikhail said. He turned and offered his hands to Emilia and Carrie. They walked back to the inn, clutching each other's hands in support.

* * *

Back inside, the three of them sat on Carrie's bed. Mikhail looked into Emilia's face as if her were searching for answers.

"Emilia," Carrie said, "did you really just assume power over the dybbuks?"

"Yes," she replied.

"Are you now their queen?" she asked incredulously.

"I suppose I am."

"Your entire life," Mikhail said, "you always swore you would never do this. You always said that when the time came, you would forsake your right to power."

He leaned into her and put a comforting arm around her shoulders.

"I know, my friend," Emilia said. "But I see now that this may have been a mistake. Did we not discuss this already in the square?"

"We did," Mikhail conceded. "I just want to make sure you are certain in your choice. I am worried about the effect this will have on you."

"I know," Emilia said. She patted Mikhail on the knee. "Please do not worry. I know I have you, and Carrie, and Ferne to keep me grounded. Soon, I shall also have Lindsay and Rebecca."

Carrie nodded. "Yes," she said. "Tomorrow we shall find the shretelech, and they will help me find my friends." She turned to Mikhail. "What do we need to do to find them?"

"We shall need things to make an offering to them," Mikhail said. "This will show we are friends to them and wish them no harm. We shall bring food and spirits. When they come out, we must approach quietly and reverently. Then we may make our request." He looked at Carrie earnestly. "Know that they are free to turn us down. We cannot force them to do as we ask."

"I understand," Carrie said.

"However, I feel it would be in our best interest to be well rested for this meeting," Mikhail said. "We have all had a trying day and night."

"I agree," Emilia said. "You are not upset with me?"

"No," Mikhail said.

"No," Carrie agreed. "I think we're just concerned. We care about you a lot. We only want what's best for you."

"Thank you," Emilia said with a small smile. She yawned. "I think I should get some sleep." She rose and went to the door, turning back; she looked once more at her friends. "I am so lucky to have people like you on my side. I want you to know how much I appreciate your friendship." She left the room, and they heard her door open and close.

Mikhail turned to Carrie. "I am worried about her," he said. "I hope she knows what she is doing."

"I'm sure she wouldn't have done what she did if she felt she had another choice," Carrie told him. "We'll look after her." On an impulse, she leaned in and drew Mikhail in for a hug. She felt his warmth against her and instantly relaxed. "We'll find my friends, right?"

"We shall do all we can," Mikhail said. "I can promise you that much."

Chapter Twenty-One:
Ha Shretele

The kitchen was abuzz with activity as Carrie, Mikhail, and Emilia prepared for their journey into the forest. Mikhail had told Mina what he would need, and she had set about finding it all for him. Soon, she procured a small honey cake and a silver flask filled with what she assured him was the best brandy the town had to offer. The man who ran the pub was all too happy to part with it as a token of gratitude to the people who had helped rid the town of the dybbuk's torture. She then packaged these things up in a small leather pouch and handed them to Mikhail.

He, Carrie, and Emilia rode through town toward the forest. It seemed to Carrie that everyone came out to greet them as they passed by. Men and women, old and young, children carrying their toys and dolls all stood outside their homes, waving and smiling as they rode past. Gone were the strained and tired eyes; everyone had a touch more colour in their cheeks. Carrie was gratified to see the good a night's peaceful sleep had done for the citizens of Shkalo. She hoped that soon her friends could be counted among the saved.

It was not long before the clip clop of their horses' hooves on cobblestone streets gave way to the smoother, quieter ride across the grass, and Carrie was once more under a large canopy of branches and leaves. She found she much preferred the sights, sounds, and smells of the forest to those of the towns and villages. There was a peacefulness here that soothed her nerves. They rode on in silence. Mikhail had told them before departing that he felt they should be as quiet as possible on their ride so as not to frighten away anyone who may be in the trees or bushes. Eventually, they made their way to a small glade. Carrie could see a clear pond, the water reflecting the trees and sparkling in the sun. The grass was dotted with bright yellow buttercups and fresh white daisies. Mikhail raised his hand to bring them to a stop, and they dismounted. Carrie watched as he took the pouch and opened it up. Finding a flat rock, Mikhail laid out the cake and flask atop the rock, using the pouch as a small makeshift tablecloth. He looked out over the glade, as if searching for a sign.

"This is for my friends the shretelech," he quietly murmured, and turned and walked back to Carrie and Emilia. "Now we sit and wait."

Carrie made herself comfortable sitting in the grass, leaning casually against the base of a tree. She could feel the warmth of her two friends on either side of her. No one spoke. They all enjoyed the silence of each other's company. Carrie closed her eyes, listening to the hum of some insects lazily flying past. She heard the occasional croak of a frog swimming in the small pond. A few birds chirped in the branches overhead. Carrie could see the sun slowly going down through the leaves in the trees. She sighed and allowed herself to completely relax for the first time in days. She thought she must have dozed off, because suddenly she felt herself being poked sharply in the ribs by Emilia. She opened her eyes a crack to see her friend's violet eyes sparkling with suppressed laughter.

"You were snoring," Emilia said softly.

"I do not snore," Carrie retorted indignantly.

"Than you were growling loudly in your sleep," Emilia amended, her eyes alight with humour.

"Exactly," Carrie said with a smile. She was delighted to see the princess smiling and joking after the events of the night before.

Mikhail clutched Carrie's arm tightly. "Shh!" he hissed. "Look!" He pointed to the rock.

Carrie looked and barely stifled a gasp. A nut-brown hand, barely the size of a small child's, was reaching up to grasp at the cake. Soon, she could see the rest of the creature as it clambered up onto the rock. Carrie's eyes went wide as she saw a shretele for the first time. He had a tiny, thin, naked body, all gangly limbs, with feet that seemed far too large for his body. His figure was topped by a round head with cherubic cheeks and giant green eyes. He had wispy, dark brown hair, full lips, a small upturned nose, and two ears ending in perfect little points. His eyes were alight with mischief, and Carrie grinned as she watched him nibble at the cake with obvious enjoyment, smacking his lips together as he sampled the brandy in the flask.

Mikhail rose slowly and began walking toward the shretele. The creature paused in his eating and looked shrewdly at the tall man approaching him. He cocked his head to the side as if considering whether or not to flee.

"Hello, friend," Mikhail said in a low voice.

The shretele nodded in greeting and resumed his feast.

"I am a friend of your people," Mikhail said. "Your kind has helped my father and me each year with our apple harvest. In return, we have gifted you with many things. I come to you now desperately seeking your help. Will you listen?"

The shretele considered Mikhail's question, then settled cross-legged on the rock, gesturing for Mikhail to continue. Mikhail sat down on the ground facing him.

"My two companions and I are seeking something," Mikhail said. "Carrie," he gestured to where she sat, "had two of her dear friends stolen by the dybbuks. We seek to get them back. We were told that they were trapped in Asmodeus' mirror. This mirror has since vanished. I know that the shretelech are masters of finding that which is lost. Can you help us?"

The shretele seemed deep in thought. He rubbed his head and tugged his ear. "We have always been enemies of the dybbuks," he said, in a voice that seemed far too deep to be coming from his tiny body. "I see you travel with one," he pointed at Emilia, "yet, she radiates kindness. I read sincerity in her. You speak truthfully about being a friend of my people. Anything that will end the dybbuks' tyranny I will help with. Yes, I will do as you ask. Give me until sunset tomorrow. I will return here, and you will bring me more of this cake and brandy. I will tell you then if I have found what you seek."

Carrie slowly stood and approached them. "Thank you," she said sincerely. "You can't know how much this means to me."

The shretele nodded. "These friends are quite dear to you, are they not?" he asked her.

"Yes," Carrie said. "They're like family to me."

"I understand," he said. "I will return tomorrow." He turned and vanished soundlessly into the trees.

Carrie turned to Mikhail. "Do you think he can do it?" She hardly dared to hope.

"If anyone can locate the mirror," he said, "it is one of the shretelech."

"Thank you," Carrie told him.

"I have done nothing," Mikhail protested.

"You had this idea," Carrie insisted. "We didn't know what to do, and you thought of asking him. So, thank you."

"Then, you are welcome," Mikhail said with a smile. "I only hope he can do as we asked him."

"As do I," Emilia said. She seemed pensive and troubled.

Carrie walked over to her and put her arm around her slender shoulders. "He was right, you know," she said.

"Hmm?" Emilia said. "About what?"

"About you," Carrie answered. "About what kind of person you are. You are kind and sincere. You do want to do so much good in this world. Otherwise, I highly doubt that Mikhail and I would want to be friends with you."

"She is right," Mikhail said.

"Thank you," Emilia told them. "I appreciate this. Now we should return to Shkalo. We will need to get more cake and brandy for the shretele's return. While there, we can see about more supplies, in the event that we need to travel to get to my father's mirror."

"Goody," Carrie said drily. "More waiting."

Mikhail laughed as he got their horses. "At least we are now waiting for someone friendly."

"At least there's that," Carrie agreed. She pulled herself into her saddle and turned her horse in the direction of Shkalo. She did not know how she would last waiting until nightfall the next day. She was filled with trepidation knowing that even if the shretele was able to find the mirror, they had no idea how to get her friends out of it, or even if they were truly inside. She took a deep breath and followed her friends back to town. She had one more day to kill.

Chapter Twenty-Two:
Lachazor

A large group of smiling people greeted Carrie, Emilia, and Mikhail upon their return to Shkalo. Carrie was once again struck by how different everyone looked. Their sombre black clothing had been replaced by dresses and tunics of all shades and colours. Their faces were transformed by a restorative night's sleep and a little hope for happiness. Where once the citizens had seemed stooped and weary, now many of them stood straight and tall. It was as if a collective weight had been lifted from their shoulders. Now everyone in Shkalo could breathe easier and live free of fear.

As Carrie and her friends rode through town, she could see a flurry of activity everywhere she turned. Everyone was hard at work, cleaning, washing windows, and tending gardens. It seemed they were all anxious to return the town to its former state of glory. Windows were once again sparkling in the sunlight. Flowers were watered and starting to perk up once more. Store signs were cleaned and glossy. Each door's brass handle or knob was buffed and gleaming. Just seeing the difference they had made warmed Carrie's heart and gave her hope. If they could change the lives of these people and help them, surely they could achieve anything they put their minds to. To her, this meant hope for Lindsay and Rebecca.

Carrie drew her horse into a stop as she approached Mina's inn. She dismounted and tied him to the hitching post that stood out in front. A little blonde girl ran up to her, clutching a collection of posies in her chubby little hand. She nervously thrust them out at Carrie. Carrie smiled warmly and took the flowers.

"Thank you," Carrie said to her, "they're lovely."

"My mother is smiling again," she said. "I picked them for you to say thank you. They are for your friends also."

"What's your name?" Carrie asked her.

The girl stared down at her feet and mumbled her answer. "Melanie." She seemed so nervous and shy.

"That's a lovely name," Carrie said. "Thank you again for the flowers, Melanie."

Emilia and Mikhail rode up to join them, and, as Melanie saw them approach, she ran off. Carrie smiled at her retreating figure. She had been like that as a child herself. She remembered finding adults so large and intimidating. She figured that it had probably taken that little girl every ounce of courage she had to come up to her with the flowers. She had probably waited for Carrie to be relatively alone, due to the fact that of the three of them, she was smallest and least intimidating to a child's perspective.

"Who was that?" Mikhail asked.

"Her name is Melanie," Carrie said. "She brought us flowers as a thank you."

Emilia took the small bouquet and sniffed them. "They are nice," she said. "If I hang them upside down inside, I can dry them so they will keep permanently. Would you like that?"

"It would be nice to have a reminder of this place," Carrie said. "Sure. Let's do that."

They went inside, and Carrie watched as Emilia divided up the flowers into three equal bunches. She tied each with some string and hung them in one of the windows.

"So," Carrie said. "What do we need to do while we wait for the shretele?"

"We need to go to the pub," Mikhail replied. He began ticking things off on his fingers. "We need some more brandy. We need another honey cake, some more clothes. I noticed that one of the tents has a tear. We either need a new one, or to get this one repaired. We are low on food and need to refill our water skins before we depart once more. I would greatly prefer to achieve this now, in anticipation of the fact that we may need to travel in order to get to the mirror. I strongly doubt the shretele will bring it to us. If it is as dangerous as everyone says, he will not want to move it." He looked at Carrie with a small twinkle in his eye. "I also feel we should have extra rations due to the fact that we may have an extra two people with us when we return to the palace."

Carrie could not suppress the grin that stretched across her face. "I so hope you're right!"

"Would you like to accompany me around town?" Mikhail asked, offering her his arm.

"I would love to," Carrie said, looping her arm through his. She turned to Emilia. "You coming with us?"

"No," Emilia said with a smile. "I think I shall stay here and pack up our belongings."

"Oh," Carrie said. "Okay, if you're sure."

"I am," Emilia answered. "You two have fun."

On their way out the door, Emilia handed Carrie a small pouch of coins. "Just in case," she said. "I know you have no money from our world."

"Thank you," Carrie replied.

* * *

Carrie found it immensely enjoyable to walk through the town on Mikhail's arm. He pointed things out to her as they walked, explaining how the windows were made, the construction of the buildings. He had learned many things from his father growing up. Carrie learned that the house Mikhail had grown up in had been built from the ground up by his father. Mikhail had learned from an early age how to hold a hammer, put up walls, thatch a roof, and lay a floor. Carrie loved hearing how things were done in Hadariah. She found hearing about building was much like learning about building the sets for the shows she worked on, the main difference being the sets she had helped build throughout high school never needed to last much longer than the play's run. A house had to withstand the test of time, and the battery of the elements.

Everywhere they went, the two of them were hailed as heroes. Carrie found it a little disconcerting. She kept pointing out that she had barely done anything; the main credit should go to Emilia. After all, it had been the princess who truly stopped the dybbuk. Yet the people of the town seemed insistent that her desire to help them was worthy of praise, whether or not she had actually been the one to personally vanquish the dybbuk that terrorized the town. She found herself blushing more and more with every encounter. Mikhail seemed to be taking it all in stride, affably conversing with everyone who came up to them. Soon, they had all they required. Shopkeepers were taking supplies to the inn for them. A new tent was given as a gift to thank them for what they had done. The pub owner was supplying them with a new flask of brandy, and the baker promised to bring them the best and freshest honey cake he could possibly make.

On their way back to the inn, Carrie noticed a small shop. She went over and peered in the window. It looked like the type of place that sold a hodgepodge of odds and ends. She could see candles, books, stones, and various pieces of jewelry lying out on tables that littered the shop from one end to the other. She turned to Mikhail with a smile.

"Can we go in here?" she asked him. "We have everything we need, and we still have some time."

"You do not need my permission to do anything, Carrie," Mikhail laughed.

Carrie ran into the shop and began exploring. Soon, it became clear that this shop was almost like an apothecary's. Everything sold seemed to have a mystical connotation to it. There were books on healing and bundles of herbs, the rocks were crystals, and the necklaces she had seen were medallions with symbols on them. Carrie browsed, fascinated. Mikhail followed close behind, seeming amused by Carrie's rapt interest in all she saw. She would ask him questions about everything, what it did, what the symbols meant. He answered all he could.

Mikhail soon wandered off on his own, saying he wanted to see about some healing herbs for their journey and that he thought it might be a good idea to have some on hand. Carrie continued her exploration of the shop and soon found something that made her eyes widen in excitement. She snatched up a large, heavy-looking chamtzah. It seemed to be made out of silver, and it dangled from a heavy chain. In the centre of the palm-shaped amulet was a large blue stone. She looked around for a shopkeeper. Seemingly out of nowhere, a wizened old woman approached. Carrie wondered where she had been while she was wandering the store.

"May I help you?" the woman asked.

Carrie felt awkward standing before her. The woman was so hunched with age, Carrie had to peer down to look her in the eye. Carrie was uncomfortably reminded of the crone she had traded her own chamtzah with in exchange for a *shamir*. Knowing that the crone had been Asmodeus in disguise made her distinctly uneasy. However, this woman seemed to be friendly.

"Yes," Carrie said, "um, how much is this?"

"For you," the woman said, "it is nothing. Take it as a gift."

"I can't," Carrie said. "That's way too generous."

"Please, take it," the woman insisted. "You have done so much for us. Let me do this for you."

"I can't," Carrie said. "Let me give you something for it."

"I will take no more than two silver coins," the woman said. "If you try to make me take any more than that, I will be horribly insulted."

"All right," Carrie agreed. She reached into her pouch and withdrew two small coins. They were the only ones that appeared silver. She knew the woman was taking far less than the necklace was worth, but she also knew when she should stop arguing. She did not want to offend her.

The woman placed the coins in the pocket of her skirt, put the necklace in a velvet pouch, and handed it back to Carrie. Mikhail reappeared from behind a bookcase with pouches of herbs and a book on healing potions. He began asking the woman about prices, and she brushed him off, insisting he take everything for free. He tried to argue as Carrie did, but she turned and walked away, effectively ending any argument he could have with her. He called a thank you at her retreating form, and he and Carrie left the shop.

"What did you buy?" Mikhail asked, seeing Carrie's small bag.

Carrie blushed crimson. "I—It's for you," Carrie stammered. "The one you have on, it's well, a little girly, and I saw this one, and it seemed nice, and I thought you would like it. Here," she said, thrusting the bag in his direction.

Mikhail took the bag, and Carrie took what he was holding so he could open it. He pulled out the chamtzah and looked at it in wonder.

"It is beautiful," he said. "Thank you. I do not know what to say."

Carrie let out a gasp of surprise as he scooped her up in a tight embrace. "You like it?"

"It is perfect."

In a move that shocked her completely, he took her face in his hands and gave her a quick kiss on the mouth. Carrie stood as if frozen, her eyes open wide. Mikhail looked away.

"I am sorry," he said. "I should not have...I mean...I acted rashly. Forgive me."

"No," Carrie said. "I mean I liked it. I mean, um, it was nice?" She was so embarrassed.

"You are not upset?" Mikhail said in surprise.

"No. I'm not upset," Carrie assured him. "I've kind of been wanting you to do that." She realized this was true and smiled up at him. "I like you. A lot."

Mikhail's face was flooded with relief. "And I, you," he said. He removed the chamtzah Carrie had lent him, replacing it with the new one. "Thank you again for the gift."

"You're welcome," Carrie said. She reached out and took his hand. Together, they returned to the inn.

Chapter Twenty-Three:
Erev

Carrie and Mikhail entered the inn still holding hands. Emilia entered the parlour and caught sight of them. Carrie saw her friend's eyes zero in on their hands and watched the smile blossom across her face.

"How was your walk?" Emilia asked, her features blandly innocent.

"Fine," Mikhail mumbled. He pulled his hand from Carrie's and hightailed it out of the room, staring at his feet the entire time.

"He is so cute when he gets flustered," Emilia giggled. "I like his necklace. Am I correct to assume this was your doing?"

"Yes," Carrie said. She felt the back of her neck grow hot. She knew her face must look beet red.

"You are both so sensitive!" Emilia crowed. She lowered her voice to a conspiratorial whisper. "Has he kissed you yet?"

"Emilia!" Carrie said. She looked away, her face flushed with embarrassment.

"He did!" Emilia exclaimed, clapping her hands with excitement. "I had so hoped he would."

Carrie stared at her friend. It dawned on her in an instant. "You stayed behind on purpose!" she accused. She wagged her finger angrily at her friend. "This whole time, you've been playing matchmaker. You did this! Don't you dare bother denying it. I'm onto you!"

"Yes, I did," Emilia said, a smug smile on her face. "I am quite good, am I not?" She batted her eyes in Carrie's direction. "Are you angry with me?"

Carrie stared as Emilia tried to paint herself as the picture of perfect innocence. However, her violet eyes were wide and full of mischief. She had attempted a pout, but the corners of her lips were quirking upwards in a small smile. Carrie began to laugh.

"I'm not mad," Carrie said. "I'm so happy. He's an amazing guy. Thank you. Neither of us would've probably tried anything without a little push."

"Good," Emilia said. "I am delighted. Now we should probably have supper. It will soon be time to go back and meet with the shretele."

Carrie felt a small shiver of anticipation. "Today just flew past," she said. "I was dreading it before. I had no idea how I would handle the waiting. Now it's almost over."

"You are apprehensive."

"Yeah," Carrie admitted, "I am. I just really hope that the shretele was able to help us. I don't know what we're going to do if he wasn't." She stood and picked nervously at the hem of her top. "Shouldn't we get Mikhail if we're going to have supper?"

"Yes, we should," Emilia answered. She put her hand on Carrie's shoulder and looked her in the eye. "Do not worry," she told her. "You must have faith. Do you mind if I go and get Mikhail? I am afraid I embarrassed him earlier. I would like to apologize."

Carrie let out a small laugh. "Go ahead," she said. "I'll meet you guys in the kitchen."

* * *

Carrie was helping Mina set the table for supper. She had just finished putting the plates out and was working on the knives and forks when Emilia and Mikhail entered. She and Mikhail exchanged shy smiles, and Emilia giggled as Mikhail gave Carrie a shy wave. He walked over and took the cutlery from Carrie to finish the job as Carrie went to get glasses from Mina.

Soon they were all sitting around the table. Mina had made them a fresh chicken potpie with a crisp green salad, lightly dressed with homemade honey vinaigrette. Carrie savoured every bite of the moist chicken surrounded by fresh root vegetables and creamy sauce. She absolutely loved the flaky crust, which tasted almost like a dessert for dinner. The salad tasted as though each leaf of lettuce and each tomato was freshly picked that day, which, according to their hostess, they were. The group of four ate in companionable silence. Throughout the meal, Carrie kept spying Mikhail trying to catch her eye. Each time, she could feel herself blush and would smile at him, causing his face to go red. Emilia seemed ecstatic by this development. Carrie knew the princess had conspired to get them together, and she seemed delighted to be witnessing the fruits of her labour.

"So you will be leaving after this meal?" Mina asked, breaking the silence.

"We will be heading back into the forest," Emilia answered.

"Will you be returning afterwards?" Mina asked.

"I do not know," Mikhail said. "It seems unlikely. If we receive information that will aid us in our quest to save Carrie's friends, we will have to act on it quickly. We will probably head wherever that knowledge leads."

"Then we shall have to say goodbye sooner rather than later," Mina said. She seemed upset by this news. She frowned and began pushing her food around on her plate.

"We'll miss you as well," Carrie said. "But we still have the rest of this meal. Also, when all this is over, we'll be back. We'll visit you." She was surprised at how upset she was over the prospect of leaving Shkalo. She had been so fearful to set foot in the town, and now she found herself a part of its people. She was saddened to be leaving them so soon.

Mina smiled. "I am glad. I will look forward to your return."

The rest of supper passed by with lots of stories and future plans of visits to Shkalo, the palace, and Emilia's castle. Mina seemed extremely excited to see both. She had never before left her town, and the prospect of travel to new and foreign lands intrigued her. When Carrie said she could come to see her in her world, Mina was positively giddy with happiness. Dessert was brought out, and they sat drinking cups of bitter coffee and eating plates of ginger cookies sprinkled with brown sugar. When the last crumb had been eaten, Mikhail looked out the window at the darkening sky.

"We should go," he said, pushing himself back from the table.

The three women followed suit. Carrie and Mikhail went to gather their bags, while Emilia opted to stay behind and help Mina clear the table and rinse out the dishes. Upstairs, Carrie and Mikhail carefully checked each room to make sure nothing was left behind.

"So, Emilia apologized?" Carrie said, as she kneeled down and looked under her bed. She rolled her eyes at her own thoughtlessness as she snagged a lone sock that was lurking under there.

"Yes, though I do not know why she felt she needed to," Mikhail said. "I was embarrassed by the fact that she knew so easily. Not that I am embarrassed by what we did," he quickly amended. "Are you?"

Carrie picked herself up off the floor clutching the offending sock. "No," she said, "I'm not. Are we...together?"

"In what way?" Mikhail asked, going through a dresser.

"In the way that, we, well, umm..." Carrie faltered. She was always terrible at these things. "Are we in a relationship?"

"Do you mean a romantic relationship?"

"Umm, okay?"

"If you want to be," Mikhail said. He looked so hopeful; Carrie felt her heart melt.

"I would like that," Carrie said. She was happy, yet she was also scared. She had so many questions about what this meant for her and him. "Can I ask you something?"

"Of course," Mikhail said.

"I live in another world," Carrie said. "I think this kind of redefines the term 'long distance relationship.' Do you think we can make this work?"

"I think we can try," Mikhail said. He smiled at her and took her hand. "We can talk about this when we have dealt with everything else we have to face. But know that I do not look at this as a major obstacle. It is no different than being with someone from a different town. In fact, depending on what ways we use to travel, it may even be closer."

Carrie smiled sheepishly. He made everything seem so simple. "Okay," she said. "We can talk more later." She looked around the room. "Do we have everything?"

"I believe so," Mikhail said. "We really need to be on our way."

Holding tightly to each other's hands, they made their way downstairs to rejoin their friends.

* * *

Mina cried as they left. She had given them all tight hugs and care packages filled with her baking. They promised several times that they would return and visit often, and had been given the same promise in return. They had then mounted their horses and rode off toward the clearing at a brisk pace. Mikhail's keen sense of direction got them there just as the sun was finishing its descent in the sky. He quickly set up the cake and flask on the same rock and settled next to Carrie and Emilia to wait for the shretele's return.

Time trickled slowly by. Carrie could feel herself growing impatient. She did not remember it being like this the last time. By the time the sun had set and a full moon was slowly making its way across the sky, Carrie was becoming restless. She sat fidgeting nervously with her necklace, winding the chain around her fingers.

"He's late," she said aloud. "Maybe he's not coming at all."

"He will be here," Mikhail assured her. "He gave his word."

A slight rustling in the grass alerted them to something approaching the rock. Carrie sat stock-still. She strained her eyes trying to see what was there by the light of the moon. She let out a disappointed breath as a small brown rabbit hopped past the rock and continued in their direction. The rabbit came to a stop before them, its little nose twitching rapidly.

"I come on behalf of my friend," the rabbit said. "He says he had a meeting with the people in the glen. He is coming, but was waylaid on his journey. He has found that which you seek and will tell all when he arrives."

Carrie let out an exclamation of relief. "Thank goodness," she said. She looked down at the little rabbit. "Have you come far?" she asked. "We have some vegetables in our pack if you're hungry."

The rabbit peered up at her with big dark eyes. "Thank you," the rabbit said. "You are most kind. That would be much appreciated."

Carrie rose and rifled through her pack. She returned with a carrot and presented it to the rabbit, who immediately set to eating it as if he had been starving for days. When he had finished, he nodded at the trio and hopped off into the woods. Carrie, Emilia, and Mikhail resumed their vigil.

"What do you think happened?" Carrie said. "Do you think he's okay?"

"I believe so," Emilia answered. "The rabbit said he was still coming. If something was terribly wrong, he would not be on his way."

Mikhail nodded in agreement. "This is true," he said. "Although, I am concerned by the fact that he was delayed at all. The shretelech are known for their punctuality and keeping true to their word. It must have taken something fairly nasty or important to cause him to be so late."

They sat for a while longer. Emilia leaned against Carrie, and Carrie allowed her head to rest on Mikhail's shoulder. His warmth and presence kept her calm. The three of them sat like this in silence, allowing their friendship to comfort themselves and give hope.

Emilia was the first to see the movement by the rock. "Look!" she breathed.

Carrie squinted, barely making out the diminutive figure struggling to climb up onto the rock. She was up and moving before Mikhail could stop her. She reached the rock in a few bounding steps, calling out a word of greeting to the shretele. When she finally saw him up close, she faltered, eyes wide in shock. He looked as if he had been in a large fight with a band of thugs. One eye was nearly swollen shut, the dark bruise spreading out over his skin like a stain. His lower lip was split down the middle, and his entire naked body was covered in an assortment of abrasions and bruises.

"Are you okay?" Carrie asked softly, kneeling down to look him in the eye. She heard Emilia and Mikhail come up behind her.

"I shall be all right," the shretele assured her. "Just give me time to catch my breath and eat a little."

Carrie nodded and sat down on the grass. She watched him nibble at the cake and take long sips of the brandy, wincing when the alcohol touched the cut on his lip. Finally, he finished and looked up at Carrie and her friends.

"There is much that is bad about this business," he said. "Things are not as they appear."

"What do you mean?" Mikhail asked.

"I located the mirror," the shretele said. "It is being guarded by a small band of dybbuks. They saw me, and it was they who gave me my injuries. They are guarding it with a human male." He turned to Carrie. "Your friends are trapped within. I heard them say as much, but they seem to expect you to come for them. They were laughing about it. This whole affair does not sit well with me."

Carrie frowned. "This sounds weird," she said. "Why would a human be helping the dybbuks?"

"I do not know for certain," the shretele said. "He mentioned a child. He said that the dybbuks must uphold their end of the bargain and keep his child safe."

"Where is the mirror?" Emilia asked. "I have assumed control over the dybbuks, taking my father's place. Maybe I can get them to step aside."

The shretele shook his head. "I was under the impression that they had a ruler," he said. "It was not you. I would tread carefully and not rely on your power."

"Where is it?" Emilia asked again.

"It is in the village of Choshech," the shretele said.

Mikhail frowned. "That's the village at the base of the Mountain of Darkness," he said. "My people would never help the dybbuks."

"Well one man is," the shretele insisted. "His house is right at the base. He works the orchard. It is his house the dybbuks are keeping the mirror in."

Mikhail's eyes went wide with horror. "No!" he said angrily. "You are wrong. That's my father's house! He would never do that."

"If this is so," the shretele said calmly, "then you must be the child he is speaking of. He thinks he is keeping you safe. He did this for you."

Chapter Twenty-Four:
Konflikt

Mikhail was pacing the glen, hands in his hair as if he were trying to tear each strand out by the root. Both Carrie and Emilia had tried to calm him down, but their efforts were violently shrugged off.

"This is impossible," Mikhail said. "My father despises the dybbuks. He was even opposed to our friendship, Emilia. Do you remember?"

"I do," Emilia answered in a calm and even tone. "However, there can be many reasons for this. Mikhail, please listen. He may be possessed. He may be doing this in some deluded belief that you are in danger. The shretele said he mentioned you."

Mikhail waved this off. He turned to the shretele, a pleading look in his eyes. "Are you certain?" he asked. "Are you certain it was the man who works the orchard?"

The shretele looked at Mikhail, eyes full of sadness. "I am certain," he said. "They called him by his name—Loren."

Mikhail's face went white. It was clear he could deny it no longer.

Carrie went over to him and put her hand gently on his arm. "If it is your father," she reasoned, "we can talk to him and get the mirror. He will listen to you. Right?"

"I do not know anymore," Mikhail said in a low voice. "I thought I knew him...I was clearly wrong. What am I to do?"

"We are to do what we have always set out to do," Emilia said brusquely. "We are to go get the mirror and save Lindsay and Rebecca. This does not change that mission." She glanced sharply at Mikhail. "I am right in this. This changes nothing."

Mikhail nodded sadly. Carrie felt her heart break for him. She knew this must be killing him inside. She loved both of her parents dearly; to have either of them betray her so severely would be a devastating blow. She could not even imagine how this must feel. "This does change things," she said quietly.

Emilia looked at her in confusion. "What? How?"

"This changes part of our goal," Carrie said. "We now have three people to save. Even if we are saving Mikhail's father from himself. He's made a terrible mistake. It may have been for the most noble of reasons. We don't know. What we do know is that he needs our help as well."

Mikhail looked gratefully at Carrie. He mouthed a silent thank you in her direction. She smiled at him and took his hand.

"You are right," Emilia said. "I am sorry, Mikhail. I sometimes forget myself. This is why I need you and your friendship. All of you."

"It is all right," Mikhail said. "I know that you would never let real harm come to anyone."

The shretele had sauntered over to their packs while all this was happening. He approached them with a small handful of herbs.

"May I have these?" he asked. "They will speed my recovery."

"Of course," Mikhail said. "If you need anything else, just ask."

"No," the shretele said. "These will do. I will be leaving you now."

With that, the shretele vanished. Carrie stared in wonder at the spot where he had previously stood. In spite of everything she had seen, magic still astonished her.

"I wish we could do that," she said. "It would certainly cut down on our travel time."

Mikhail laughed. "Yes, well we shall have to ride. It is at least a day's journey from here. Should we head back to Shkalo for the night, or stay here?"

"I think we should stay here," Carrie said after a moment's consideration. "If we go back now, Mina will probably be asleep. Our knocking on her door would scare her. Everyone in that town desperately needs their rest."

"Carrie is right," Emilia said. "Let us set up camp here. We have flat ground and clean water. This spot looks safe enough for one night."

"Okay," Mikhail agreed. He went to go get the tents set up.

Emilia watched him go and turned to Carrie. "You are good for him," she said. "Thank you for what you are doing."

"What do you mean?" Carrie asked, looking at Emilia with concern.

"You do realize there is a very real chance we might not be able to save his father, don't you?" Emilia asked.

"Why not?" Carrie said. She could feel her heart pound in her chest. She refused to lose anyone else to the dybbuks.

"If we save your friends," Emilia explained, "the dybbuks may see it as a failure on Mikhail's father's part. At the worst, it will be betrayal. They will not hesitate to kill him."

"But you put yourself in charge!" Carrie insisted. "You can stop them."

"Only if they recognize my power," Emilia said. "The shretele made it clear they all do not. It seems that I may have caused a rift in their factions. Some see my rejection of my father's ways as a betrayal of them all."

Carrie shook her head. "What do we do?"

"We do our best," Emilia said. "That is all we can do. Hopefully we can save them all. Just know there is a very real chance we cannot."

* * *

That night, Carrie lay under her blankets tossing and turning. Her dreams ranged from the unsettling to the frightening. She dreamed her parents were possessed. Her father and mother chased her down endless hallways of mirrors. Their eyes were red and glowing with a wicked fire. They called her useless, stupid, unworthy. Carrie could not escape them no matter how far or fast she ran. She begged and pleaded with them to let her go. She cried and bargained with the dybbuks to release her parents, but all she got in return was more cruel laughter and taunting.

She found herself in an empty cave. The grey, rough stone walls were eerily familiar. She heard the crackling of a fire and followed the noise. She walked through the cave's odd twists and turns, watching as the light grew brighter. She walked slowly into the main cavern, seeing a familiar cauldron bubbling over a large fire. This time, unlike her first visit to Hadariah, there were two crones hunched over the strange brew. She approached cautiously.

"Look who finally comes," the taller of the two said without even looking up. Her long, straight, wispy grey hair floated around her shoulders, waving slightly in the breeze.

"I was beginning to think she'd forgotten about us," said the other. Her shoulders were hunched, and her voice was hoarse.

Carrie moved closer. Her heart thudded with fear. She could see them more clearly now. Their faces were lined with age and crisscrossed with a nasty grid work of scars. They moved arthritically, limbs protesting with even the simplest of motions. Carrie's mouth opened involuntarily as two names rose unbidden to the tip of her tongue.

"Lindsay," Carrie sobbed. "Rebecca."

At the sound of these names, the crones' heads snapped up, and they turned to stare at Carrie. Cruel accusation was written across every feature.

"Where were you?" Rebecca wailed, pointing a gnarled finger at Carrie.

"We were suffering while you had adventures with your boyfriend!" Lindsay shrieked.

"No!" Carrie cried. "I was trying to find you! I'm coming to you! Please tell me it's not too late!"

"It was too late the moment we were taken," Rebecca snarled.

"You should've been taken with us," Lindsay hissed. "Why weren't you?"

"Why were you labeled Emilia's pet?" Rebecca asked, inching closer to Carrie. "Why were you deemed worthy of her special protection? Was it because she wanted you for her boy?"

"No," Carrie protested. "No, that's not it at all!"

A soft hand settled on Carrie's shoulder, startling her badly.

"Come away from here," said a kind and familiar voice. "Don't listen. They're full of lies."

Carrie looked up and a lump came to her throat. Smiling down on her was the loving face of her bubbie. She was speechless. The cave faded away around her, and she found herself standing in the glen, clinging to her grandmother with all her strength. She breathed in the same scent she had grown up smelling around the house—a smell of face cream and peppermint.

"Are you real?" Carrie asked, her voice muffled against her bubbie's blouse. "Are you really here? Are you an ibbur?"

"I am here," her bubbie said in a warm voice, tinted with a Polish accent. "I just wanted to give you strength. You will need it. I am so proud of you, Carraleh. You have done so much and come so far. I have been watching over you, and I'm so proud of the young woman you've become."

Carrie looked up into the smiling eyes she had missed so much. They were the very same blue-green that looked out of her mirror every day. Her bubbie's hair was the same sandy shade that Carrie knew had been supplied by her hairdresser, but was the same colour it had naturally been when she was a young woman. Everything about her was exactly as Carrie had remembered as a young girl, sitting in the kitchen, baking cookies, telling stories, talking about their days. Hearing her old nickname for her made her heart swell.

"I'm so happy to see you," Carrie said, tears in her eyes. "I've missed you so much."

"I've missed you too, *ziese*," her bubbie said. "I can't stay long, but know I love you." She smiled at her granddaughter. "I have a message for your friend Rebecca."

"What is it?" Carrie asked.

"Her bubbie wants her to know she's proud of her, too," Carrie's bubbie said. She took Carrie's hands in her own. "Tell her this when you see her. Not *if*. *When*."

Carrie sighed happily. It felt as if a massive weight had been lifted off of her shoulders. That one little word meant so much. "Thank you, Bubbie. I love you, too."

Carrie smiled in her sleep. The rest of the night passed by peacefully, and her dreams were troubled no more.

Chapter Twenty-Five:
Mefuchedet

The next morning, Carrie woke up feeling truly rested for the first time since her return to Hadariah. She greeted the sun with a smile. Emilia and Mikhail exited their tents to find Carrie already frying eggs in a pan over the fire, humming a tune as she cooked them all breakfast.

"Sleep well?" Mikhail asked.

"Yes, I did," Carrie answered. "It didn't start out that way, but I think an ibbur visited me. She told me some things that actually gave me hope. For once, it wasn't warnings and premonitions."

"What happened?" Emilia asked her.

"I started out having these horrible nightmares. They were full of horrible things. There were dybbuks, and they had taken over my parents. Lindsay and Rebecca were there again as well." Carrie shuddered at the memory. "Then my bubbie came. She told me she was proud of me and that we would find my friends and save them. It wasn't just a dream. It felt real. I woke up feeling truly hopeful for the first time in a while."

"I believe you," Mikhail told her, taking a plate of food. "It is about time we actually had some good news brought to us."

They quickly finished eating and cleaning up their campsite. Carrie made certain that their fire was out while Emilia and Mikhail packed up the tents. Soon they were once more on their way. Mikhail checked his compass to be sure they were headed in the right direction. In spite of her hopeful message, Carrie knew he was nervous. Emilia kept looking over at him, her worry was plain on her face. Carrie met her eye a few times, offering her a grim smile. If anyone understood how it felt to confront a parent, it was Emilia.

As they rode on, Carrie felt that the path they travelled seemed familiar. The more they saw, the more she became sure of it. She started looking for things that she remembered, caves she passed, large rocks she and her friends had climbed. Soon, a feeling of unease slowly started creeping up her spine. She felt her horse start to twitch nervously beneath her. She looked to her friends and saw they were feeling the same. All sound seemed to drain from the world around them. Carrie desperately wanted to cry out to them, ask them what was going on. Her hand reached up to clutch at her necklace.

"What is this place?" Carrie choked out.

"This part of the forest is enchanted," Emilia said, her voice tense. "A witch dwells nearby. She wants people to rush through her land as quickly as possible. If they do not, they will lose hope and die."

Carrie shuddered. "I remember being here the last time I was in Hadariah," she said. "It's awful. There's a river coming up ahead, though. It seemed to make everything better."

Mikhail nodded, a short jerking movement of his head. He seemed more affected by the place than either Carrie or Emilia. He nudged his heels into his horse's sides, spurring it to go faster. Carrie and Emilia followed suit. Very quickly, all three of them galloped through the trees. Carrie breathed an audible sigh of relief when the sound of water reached her ears. They broke through the last row of trees, and Carrie was able to see a familiar bridge come closer. She turned to Emilia and pointed with a smile.

"That's where we saved you before," Carrie said. She faltered at Emilia's perplexed expression. She had forgotten that the princess she and her friends had rescued two years before had actually been Asmodeus in disguise. "Oh," Carrie said, understanding finally dawning on her. "That wasn't you."

"No," Emilia said. "I was rescued by you in my father's dungeon."

"Yeah," Carrie sheepishly replied. "Sorry."

Emilia smiled kindly. "It was an honest mistake."

They slowed their horses to a walk and approached the bridge over the river. The horses balked at the start of the bridge. Carrie held tightly to her reins and tried forcing her horse to cross, but it was to no avail. Emilia and Mikhail were having the same trouble.

"What's going on?" Carrie asked. "What's wrong with the horses?"

"Did you notice anything wrong with the bridge the last time you were here?" Mikhail asked her.

"No," Carrie said. She thought hard. "Do you see that big rock in the middle of the river?" she asked, pointing towards it. "Emilia, or rather the person we thought was Emilia, was marooned on the rock. We saved her—er, him—and continued on in our travels. At the time, we'd had no idea that we were travelling with your father in disguise. It is so strange to think of it now."

"I remember that a lot of people were staying indoors during that time," Mikhail said. "Everyone was terrified."

"What are you saying?" Carrie asked, eyeing Mikhail carefully.

"Maybe this bridge is a home," Mikhail said.

Emilia looked the bridge up and down. "Let us see about this," she said. She jumped down out of the saddle and approached the bridge. She briskly knocked on the railing. "I command you to leave your nest," Emilia ordered.

Carrie and Mikhail sat and waited. A little man dressed in rags clambered over the side of the bridge. He was round and wrinkled. His brown beard was matted and had been tucked into the piece of twine he was using for a belt. He smiled up at Emilia, showing off his mouth full of rotting, razor-like teeth.

"What can I do for you, milady?" he asked, with a mocking bow.

"I demand safe crossing over this bridge," Emilia said imperiously.

"Oh ho!" he laughed. "Do you? What will you give me for it?"

"I will give you nothing," Emilia said. "Nothing but my word that I will not crush you."

"What is she doing?" Carrie hissed at Mikhail.

"I believe she is dealing with a *lante*."

"A what?"

"I believe you likened it to a creature called a 'hobgoblin,'" Mikhail explained. "They are notorious for breaking agreements and drowning people in their rivers."

"Ah," Carrie said. "I'll leave her to it then."

"How do you propose to 'crush me'?" the lante sneered at the princess.

"Do you know who I am?" Emilia asked him. "I am the Princess Emilia, daughter of Asmodeus. The girl on the horse is my dear friend Carrie. She helped destroy my father. You are nothing compared to what he was. Need I go on?"

The lante took a startled step backwards. "I was merely asking how you would do it," he said. "Of course, you may cross safely." He stepped back and showed them the way over. "Go ahead, with my blessing." He narrowed his eyes, a mischievous look on his tiny face. "Of course," he said, "there is the matter of the toll."

"Toll?" Emilia asked sharply.

"My bridge, my rules," the lante said.

"What is this toll?" Emilia demanded.

"I ask a riddle, you answer. You get it right, and you may cross—if you pay me with some sweets," the lante said with a grin.

"And if we answer incorrectly?" Emilia asked.

"Find a new way to cross," the lante said. "This has always been my arrangement."

"Very well," Emilia said. "Ask."

The lante cocked his head to the side and thought. "I grow in the woods. I hang in the shop. When you touch me, I cry. What am I?"

Emilia turned to Carrie and Mikhail. "I confess, I am confused," she said. "What do you think it is?"

"Well," Carrie said, "if it grows in the woods, maybe it's plant based."

"This is good," Mikhail said with an encouraging nod. "Once it is picked, it can hang in a shop waiting to be bought."

"Yes," Emilia said. "But how can it cry? That part has me confused."

"Take all the time you need," the lante called from his spot on the bridge. "I have all day!"

"But we don't," Carrie muttered. "Okay, so we know it grows, can be sold, makes noise." She thought for a while. Suddenly, it hit her. "I know what it is! Lante, are you a violin?"

"Very good, little girl," the lante said. "You may all pass."

Carrie reached into her pack and pulled out a fruit tart that Mina had baked for them before they left. She handed it to Emilia, who went and gave it to the lante.

"Lovely," he said. "This will do nicely. Now be on your way."

Emilia nodded. "Thank you, good sir," she said with a sweet smile. She gave him a small curtsey and went back to her horse.

Carrie, Mikhail, and Emilia crossed over the bridge, thanking the lante as they passed. Carrie heard the lante mutter something under his breath. She strained to hear and thought it sounded as if he said, "They will get theirs when they meet the tafelmusik." She shook her head at the sheer nonsense of it.

They continued on their way, chatting genially. Mikhail could not stop congratulating Carrie for her quick wit in figuring out the riddle's solution.

"It was nothing," Carrie said. "You would have figured it out eventually."

"But you did first," Mikhail said. "That was amazing."

"Thanks," Carrie said smiling at him. "Mikhail, you mentioned a bit of what it was like when the violin's strings were stolen. What happened? I only know what I saw and what Adom told me. What was it really like?"

Mikhail looked around them, at the trees, the sky, the birds. He seemed lost in thought. "Do you see all of this?" he asked. "Everything here is so alive. The plants, animals, people—everything is singing, living. It was as if someone had stolen the very soul from this world. We all felt it. It felt as if a piece of our hearts had been ripped away. Our lives felt smaller, diminished. Living where we were, my father and I could feel it the instant Asmodeus had the strings. It was almost a physical pain. We did not dare leave our home. We feared any movement we made would be perceived as a threat by the dybbuk king." He turned and looked at Emilia. "I already told you this part," he said to her. "But when Emilia stopped coming by to check on us, my father took that as a sign that all was lost. If even she could not stop him, and he could turn against his own child, there was no hope left. He was so happy when the strings were returned and life went back to normal. This is why I do not understand his actions now."

"We'll fix this," Carrie promised.

"I know you believe that," Mikhail replied.

"You're right," she answered. "I do. I did last time, too."

Mikhail smiled. "You almost have me convinced."

"She is quite convincing," Emilia chimed in. "I would fear for those who dare stand in her way."

"Small and mighty. That's me." Carrie let go of her reins and flexed her arms.

Suddenly, Carrie's horse stumbled. Carrie struggled to keep her balance in the saddle, but the horse began to buck wildly. Something had it frightened. In the instant before she was thrown, Carrie could see her friends' horses were both wild with fear, their eyes wide and staring. As she flew through the air toward the ground, her thoughts focused on one clear question: *why does my horse have human feet?*

Chapter Twenty-Six:
Hu lo Amar 'Tafelmusik'

Carrie groaned. Every limb ached. Her head pounded horribly. She decided to try opening her eyes, and the sun that shone above her only made everything ten times worse. She squinted against the light and tried turning her head away.

"She's waking up," Mikhail said. Carrie could hear the relief tinged with worry in his voice.

"Carrie," Emilia said. "Open your eyes."

"No. Too bright," Carrie mumbled.

"Please," Mikhail asked.

Carrie opened her eyes, and Emilia and Mikhail's faces swam into focus. She could read the concern on their faces. She tried to sit up, and finally managed it, cringing at the pain. She was sure she was covered in bruises.

"How long was I out?" she asked weakly.

"Several minutes," Mikhail said. "You scared us immensely."

"What hurts?" Emilia asked.

"Everything." Carrie tested her limbs, gingerly bending and straightening her arms and legs, wiggling her fingers and toes. "I don't think anything's broken. Just badly bruised."

"You were quite lucky," Mikhail said. "We feared you had hit your head on a rock. When you did not respond to us, or wake up…" He stopped talking and pulled Carrie into his arms, placing a gentle kiss on her forehead.

"I'll be okay, Mikhail," Carrie said. "I don't plan on going anywhere."

"We will not be going anywhere," Emilia said. "At least not until we fix our horses."

At the mention of the horses, Carrie pushed herself out of Mikhail's arms, wincing at the pain that moving brought. "I saw the strangest thing," she said. "As I fell, I saw the horses' feet. But it's impossible. They looked *human*."

"Look," Mikhail said, pointing.

Carrie turned her head. There stood their three horses, moving restlessly and clearly afraid. Each one of their legs ended in a man's foot. The poor animals clearly did not know what to do with their new appendages. Carrie sat staring wordlessly at the sight, mouth agape. She turned to look at her friends, as if they could somehow explain away the odd sight. However, Emilia shook her head in confusion, and Mikhail merely shrugged.

"How?" was all Carrie managed to say when she finally found her voice.

"I assume it is a spell," Mikhail said.

"But who did this?" Carrie asked. "Who *can* do this?"

"There are some witches I have heard of who do a transformation spell," Emilia answered. "However, none of them live anywhere near these parts."

Carrie turned to Mikhail. "You helped me before we entered Muzikonstin," she said to him. "Can you work some spell on the horses?"

Mikhail smiled helplessly. "What I did for you was merely a minor charm," he replied. "What is required to help these poor horses is far beyond my skill."

"Emilia?" Carrie asked. She felt bad for the animals. They looked so confused by what had happened, and she knew there was no way to explain any of it to them. She was not certain she understood it all herself.

The princess shook her head. "I have some rudimentary powers," she said. "But nothing compared to what my father had. I am only half of what he was. My mother was mortal."

Carrie looked closely at her friend. Suddenly everything about Emilia made much more sense—her confusion about her place in the world, how she seemed to understand humans far more than the subjects of her dybbuk kingdom, and her fear of assuming her position as their leader. Emilia seemed uncomfortable to speak any more about it.

"Well," Carrie said, "if it wasn't a witch, then what could it have been? Could it've been a lante, like that guy from the bridge?" As soon as she mentioned him, something twigged in her memory. But the more she tried to remember, the more her head hurt.

Mikhail's eyes narrowed in concern. "Carrie?" he asked, pulling her closer to him. "What is it?"

"The lante," Carrie said.

"He could not have been responsible," Emilia said. "He promised us safe passage. One can clearly argue that this is not safe."

"No," Carrie said. "He said something as we passed. He said that we would get ours when we meet something, or someone. I'm not sure. My head hurts."

"I will prepare something for your head," Emilia said. She grabbed some herbs from Mikhail's bag and began mixing them into Carrie's water skin.

"Do not strain yourself too much," Mikhail told Carrie. "I do not like to see you in pain."

Carrie nodded. "Thank you, Mikhail," she told him. "But if what I heard can help us, I need to remember."

Emilia handed Carrie the mixture she had made. "Drink this," she said to her friend. "It may taste dreadful, but please, drink it all."

Carrie sniffed at the drink and made a face. It smelled like rotting leaves. The prospect of actually drinking it made her stomach lurch. She took a tentative sip and gagged. Somehow, it tasted even worse than it smelled. It tasted as if she were sucking a car air freshener wrapped in somebody's used gym sock. She plugged her nose with one hand and took a larger sip. Without the smell, it went down much easier. She figured it would be better to just get it over with, and quickly downed the rest of the disgusting concoction. Once she had swallowed the last drop, she sat back and waited. Carrie felt her headache begin to subside, and she snuggled into Mikhail's side while she tried her best to remember the lante's parting words.

She felt herself relax, and as she did, the pain receded to a much more manageable level. She tried to remember. She remembered the bridge, the little man's creepy smile. She remembered his clothes, his beard. She remembered him laughing. She remembered...

"I think he said 'tafelmusik,'" Carrie said. "I think he said that we would get ours, when we meet the tafelmusik."

"There is no such creature," Mikhail said.

"I know," Carrie replied. "I took a music appreciation course in high school. That's a type of music. I must've heard wrong. Is there something that sounds like that?"

"Like tafelmusik?" Emilia said. "I don't know."

"Something that sounds like tafelmusik that has the power to make horses' feet men's feet," Mikhail said pensively. He sat and thought, absentmindedly winding his fingers through Carrie's. His eyes lit up suddenly. "What about the kapelyushniklech?" he asked.

"It's not exactly like what Carrie said," Emilia responded, "but yes, they could indeed be responsible."

Carrie thought back to her conversation with Mikhail from a few days before. She vaguely remembered what he had said about them.

"Are those the guys who love hats?" Carrie asked.

Mikhail gave a small chuckle. "Yes," he said. "They wear little caps, that some say may be the source of their power. They perform mischief and love to tease horses. They have the power to have done this."

"So if they are the most likely suspect," Carrie said, "what do we do?"

"We need to set a trap for them," Emilia said. "Once we have them, we take their hats for ransom."

Carrie nodded. This seemed like the most sensible plan. Now all they needed to do was find bait. Mikhail propped Carrie against a tree and began searching through their packs with Emilia, both discussing what was best to use. Carrie lay back and allowed their words to wash over her. She could use a moment of removing herself from all of this. Just focusing on nothing. No friends in danger, no dybbuks, no spirits. She just rested, feeling the rough bark of the tree through the thin cotton of her tunic. She felt all the aches and pains of her body, muted now, and knew that she would be terribly sore for the next few days, yet in this instant, she could not bring herself to care.

A hand on her shoulder brought Carrie back to reality. She looked up into Emilia's violet eyes. Her friend's pale face was flush with exertion.

"We have set a trap," Emilia said to her.

Carrie raised a quizzical eyebrow, prompting her friend to continue.

"We have set gold coins on the ground," Emilia said quietly. "Mikhail has set a few snares. He has done this throughout his father's orchard to stop curious animals from destroying their trees. He is quite good at it. When the kapelyushniklech come to get the gold, they will be ensnared."

"Are you sure nothing else will get caught?" Carrie asked.

"No animal has any use for gold," Emilia reasoned. "The kapelyushniklech have a love for shiny things."

Carrie nodded. Their thinking made sense to her. "Now what do we do?"

"We hide, and we wait," Emilia replied.

Chapter Twenty-Seven:
Geyeg

Mikhail and Emilia cautiously led the horses away, tying them to some trees nearby. Carrie picked herself up off the ground and walked a short distance away. She hid in some bushes, careful to ensure she still had a view of the area. She felt the leaves and branches around her stir as Mikhail and Emilia joined her. All three of them crouched there, watching where their traps had been laid.

"How long do you think it'll take?" Carrie asked in a whisper.

"I cannot tell you," Emilia answered. "It could take minutes, or even hours."

Carrie adjusted her position, trying to find a way to be comfortable as she settled in for a long wait. She carefully reached out and pulled a couple of the branches to the side, trying to afford herself a better sight line. Mikhail watched her every move, as if he were trying to reassure himself that she was all right. Carrie heard a rustling in the grass nearby. She turned her head to see what it was, but could see nothing. All three of them were holding their breath, too nervous to even make the slightest sound, not wanting to scare away whatever was approaching.

They stayed like that for what seemed like ages, muscles tense and sweat beading on their brows. The rustling grew louder and was soon accompanied by a loud snuffling. It was almost upon them. Carrie let out a nervous giggle as she finally saw what was coming by. A fat hedgehog lazily made its way into the clearing. Its rump wiggled as it walked by them, black eyes bright with curiosity as it saw the gold. Mikhail grit his teeth as he saw it walk perilously close to one of his snares, but the animal did not spring their trap. Soon, it had left the clearing, leaving everything as Emilia and Mikhail had left it. The trio breathed easier once more.

Time ticked by in what felt like dribbles and drabs. Carrie felt as if insects were crawling up her legs, but was scared to try and see, fearful of making unnecessary noise. She felt Mikhail move slightly beside her, trying to readjust his position. Emilia was slowly moving one hand, then the other, stretching her legs slightly as she did so. Carrie allowed herself to carefully turn her head from side to side, to try and prevent her neck from getting too stiff. She sighed and gave up, swatting at her legs. Emilia looked sharply at her, and Carrie gave a tiny apologetic shrug. Mikhail suddenly gave a warning hiss and they turned their attention back to their snares.

A little man, about a half-foot shorter than Carrie's five feet, had entered the area. His clothing appeared to be sewn entirely out of leaves and birch bark, with the exception of the bright red cap perched at a jaunty angle atop his mess of carrot-coloured hair. His feet were bare and fairly large compared to his spindly body. He had a long, narrow face with a nose to match. His mouth was wide with berry red lips. When he saw the gold, his eyes lit up, and he went for it with gusto, grabbing at the coins with eager little hands. It did not take long before the snare snapped around his ankle, flinging him upside down in the air. His limbs flailed for purchase, but found none. His mouth flapped open and shut, as if he were a fish gasping for breath. His eyes rolled around in his head looking for some way out of this mess.

The instant the trap was sprung, Emilia and Mikhail were on their feet and running toward it. Carrie followed at a slower pace, not wanting to aggravate her injuries. Mikhail reached the kapelyushnikle first, snapping up the cap that had fallen free of its owner's head the second he had turned upside down. He, Emilia, and Carrie stood in a row staring at their prize. The little man gnashed his teeth at them, trying to pull his face into a fearful and intimidating expression and failing miserably.

"Give me back my hat," he snarled.

"Not until you promise to do something for us first," Mikhail said.

"And what would that be?" the kapelyushnikle asked petulantly.

"Our horses were struck with a mysterious ailment," Emilia said, her face the picture of perfect innocence. "It seems that their hooves have transformed into men's feet."

The kapelyushnikle began to cackle uproariously. "That is too rich!" he cried. "That is an amazing trick. Whoever managed to do that is an impressive talent. Incredible!"

"We think it was you," Carrie drily. "Thanks to you, my horse threw me to the ground. I could've been seriously injured. Was that the point of this?"

The kapelyushnikle pouted. "I did not mean for any of you to be hurt," he said. "I was merely having fun. At your expense, of course."

"Of course," Carrie said. "Now fix it."

"If I get my hat back," he said to her.

"That can be arranged," Mikhail said.

Emilia went to retrieve the horses, leaving Carrie and Mikhail guarding the kapelyushnikle. He regarded his captors through lidded eyes. He seemed wary of them, as though sizing them up for some unknown purpose of his.

"I know who your friend is," he drawled. "I also know why you are travelling through these woods."

"Oh?" Mikhail asked, a carefully neutral expression on his face.

"Many hope you will fail," he continued. "The dybbuks who have the mirror have a purpose to what they are doing. They plan to bring the princess down. Such as me like the chaos that having no clear ruler brings to these parts. We like being able to have our fun whenever we want."

"Good luck having your fun without this," Mikhail said dangling the hat just out of reach. He watched the kapelyushnikle reach futilely for it and laughed.

"Stop it," Carrie chided him. "It's bad enough he's being forced to dangle like this. Don't tease him."

"After what he did to you?" Mikhail said. "Why do you care?"

"We shouldn't stoop to his level," Carrie said to him. "You're better than this."

Mikhail gave Carrie a sheepish look. "I am sorry," he said.

"Don't apologize to me," Carrie answered.

Mikhail nodded. "I apologize," he said to the kapelyushnikle. "I was out of line."

The kapelyushnikle gave Mikhail an upside down nod of acceptance. "Now give me my hat," he stubbornly insisted.

"When you promise to fix our horses," Mikhail said back.

Emilia returned with their horses. The animals tried to shy away upon seeing the kapelyushnikle. They tripped over their odd feet, and seemed scared and miserable. The little man began to laugh at his handiwork. Carrie was thoroughly disgusted that anyone could be amused by the horses' discomfort. She turned an angry eye to the kapelyushnikle.

"You find this funny?" she asked him incredulously.

"Oh yes," he said chuckling. "But I will fix your stupid animals."

Carrie walked over to him and pulled out her dagger. With one swipe, she cut his rope, unceremoniously dumping him on the ground in a tangled heap.

"We could have done that more gently," Mikhail murmured.

"I know," she answered with an indifferent shrug.

"What happened to not stooping to his level?"

"Nobody's perfect."

The kapelyushnikle dusted himself off and walked over to Mikhail, hand out. "Give me my hat," he said. "I cannot fix these creatures without it."

"Give me your word that you will fulfill your part of the bargain first,"

Mikhail said. "Know that if you double cross us, my friend Emilia will track you down and make you sorry you did."

The kapelyushnikle gave Emilia a considering glance. She glared at him as menacingly as she could. He nodded at Mikhail. "You have my word."

Mikhail tossed him his hat, and he placed it on his head. He looked at the horses and snapped his fingers. Instantly, the feet disappeared, and the horses were calmed as they stood once more on their hooves. Carrie turned to the kapelyushnikle and was unsurprised to see that he had vanished without a trace, along with all the gold that had been placed in their trap.

"He took our gold," she said.

"Was there ever any doubt he would?" Emilia asked as she set to work gathering their packs and placing them on their horses.

Carrie shrugged. "I shouldn't be surprised by anything anymore."

"No, you really should not be," Mikhail said, earning himself a playful swat on the arm.

Carrie got an assisting boost from Mikhail back into her saddle. She reached forward and patted her horse on the neck. "No hard feelings from before," she whispered to him. "We're good."

Mikhail and Emilia watched this exchange with a smile. They then pulled themselves up into their own saddles, and Mikhail checked his compass.

"That way," he said pointing straight ahead. "I do not believe it is much farther."

Carrie narrowed her eyes in confusion. "Why is it so short this time?" she asked. "I could've sworn it took days before."

"I believe my father was trying to make you give up by taking a long way," Emilia answered. "There are shortcuts we will employ."

Carrie nodded. "Okay. Lead on, Mikhail."

The three of them trotted off, knowing that the hardest part was yet to come, alternately filled with the desire for it all to be over, and the fear of what they had yet to face.

Chapter Twenty-Eight:
Hashiva ha Baytah

The view of the Mountain of Darkness was no less intimidating by the light of day than it had been, nearly two years before, in the never-ending darkness. Even though Carrie knew she did not have to enter the foreboding castle that sat atop its peak, she still had shivers looking up at its mighty summit. She saw Emilia and Mikhail ride on ahead and spurred her horse onward. As she approached the town of Choshech, she saw signs of life carrying on as if there was nothing wrong at all. Men and women went about their daily chores. Children chased hoops and balls down the streets, laughing and playing with each other. People called greetings to their neighbours and to both Mikhail and Emilia as they rode past. Carrie smiled as she saw how well-liked her friends were in their hometown.

"Where are we going?" Carrie asked. "I thought you told me you lived in the house closest to the mountain."

"I do," Mikhail replied. "I thought it prudent to stable the horses elsewhere and discuss our plan."

"This seems wise," Emilia said. "I noticed you were leading us farther than necessary."

"Why didn't you say anything?" Carrie asked her.

"I know Mikhail," Emilia said. "If he did not want to return home right away and face his father, I figured we should give him some time."

They continued on through town until Mikhail pulled his horse to a stop in front of the blacksmith's shop. Emilia and Carrie followed suit. Mikhail lowered himself out of his saddle and called out a greeting. A red-faced elderly man in an apron exited the shop. His jovial face broke into a delighted grin at the sight of his guests.

"Mikhail!" he cried, running a hand through his thinning grey hair.

"Wolfe!" Mikhail answered. "May my friends and I leave our horses with you? I am under the impression that my father's stable is full."

"Of course," Wolfe said. "I owe you greatly for the help you gave me last winter. Anything you need."

"Thank you, old friend," Mikhail said.

Wolfe called for his apprentice. A pock-faced boy ran out, stammered a few words of greeting, and retreated with the horses in tow. Mikhail exchanged a few more words with the blacksmith, and turned to leave. Carrie and Emilia followed as he headed off to a small restaurant. The hostess, a plump rosy woman, gave Mikhail a hug and directed them to a small private table in the back. She brought them tankards of ale and departed, leaving them alone to talk.

"So what is the plan exactly?" Carrie asked. "Do we just storm in there and demand them to hand over the mirror? 'Cause I'll tell you right now—that is probably not going to work."

Mikhail took a long swig of his ale. "I do not know," he said. "We cannot just burst in. This is true. However, this is still my home. I do not feel right sneaking in like a common thief."

"What if we did neither?" Emilia asked. She took a small sip of her drink. "What if Mikhail just went in through the front door with us? We neither burst in, nor do we sneak. We go in as if nothing is wrong."

"That's acting," Carrie said. She sounded utterly horrified. "I suck at acting. My friends always tell me I couldn't act my way out of a paper bag."

Mikhail and Emilia looked at her, identical dumbfounded expressions on their faces.

"It's an expression," Carrie said. "Just know I am an absolutely terrible actress."

"I am sorry, Carrie," Mikhail said. "Emilia's plan may be our only chance. Unless you have any better ideas?"

"No," said Carrie, sulking. "I don't."

"Okay," Emilia said. "We shall finish our drinks and be on our way."

Carrie stared at her untouched drink. She was about to face the dybbuks and her boyfriend's father. She grimaced and downed her tankard. She needed all the help she could get.

* * *

Mikhail had grown up in a sturdy little cottage with a blue front door. It had a neat little thatch roof, stone walls, and two small square windows with wooden flower boxes. Everything about the home was neat, trim, and well-built. Carrie could see that it had been put together with love and care. She looked from the cottage to Mikhail and tried to read what he was feeling, but found him to be inscrutable. It scared her how fast she had come to care for him, and she cared deeply. She knew the whole situation was troubling him, and she had no idea how to fix it. Unfortunately, right at this moment, her priority was saving Lindsay and Rebecca. Mikhail would have to come after she had them back safe and sound.

Mikhail took a deep, steadying breath and walked up to his front door. He looked over his shoulder, as if telling himself that he was not in this alone. His eyes met Emilia's, and she gave him a small smile. He looked at Carrie, and she reached out and took his hand. She felt him give her a squeeze, and she squeezed back. He turned the doorknob, and they walked in together.

The front door led them into a small room that was the parlour, kitchen, and dining room in one. Carrie looked around at the hardwood floors, yellow curtains, and dark-stained wooden furniture. The fireplace had a large, stone mantel made out of the same stone the entire home had been built from, and a small fire was dying slowly in the hearth. On either side of the fireplace was a door. Mikhail pointed them out, explaining that the one on the left was his father's bedroom. The right led to his room. As she looked, Carrie realized with a twinge of disappointment that nowhere did she see a mirror.

Suddenly, the door on the left opened, and a man walked out. Carrie surmised that this must be Mikhail's father. He resembled his son in many ways. Carrie took in the same tall stature, same long limbs, same lightly curling dark hair, and same wide eyes. However, that was where the similarities ended. Where Mikhail's eyes were grey, Loren's were a dark shade of green. Where Mikhail's face was smooth, this man's was creased with age and worry. His dark hair was liberally streaked with silver, and he was developing a slight stoop when he walked. When he saw his son, his eyes widened in fear, and his hands started to shake. Carrie could see concern written across his face, deepening the lines etched there.

"Mikhail," Mikhail's father said. It came out almost like a moan of pain. "Why have you come home?"

"Cannot a boy come home to see his father?" Mikhail asked feigning happiness. "I missed you. As did Emilia."

"Hello, sir," Emilia said with a dainty curtsey.

"I also have someone I wish you to meet," Mikhail continued. He pulled Carrie out from behind him. "This is Carrie. I met her recently, and in that short time, she has become quite dear to me. I truly believe you will like her. Carrie, this is my father, Loren."

Carrie blushed a deep shade of red. She tried to curtsey as Emilia had, and knew it looked terribly off kilter. She was still stiff and sore from her fall. "Hello, sir," she said, parroting Emilia's greeting. "I am very pleased to meet you. Mikhail has told me many wonderful stories of his childhood."

Carrie could see pain flash in Mikhail's father's eyes. He turned back to his son. "You must leave now," he said urgently. "Please."

"Why, Father?" Mikhail asked innocently. "If something is wrong we can help. Please tell me what we can do."

Loren shook his head. "No," he said. "I do not want you here. You must get out now."

"You do not mean that," Mikhail said. "Tell me what is happening."

"You know what is happening," Loren said angrily. "Do not presume I am stupid. I am your father, Mikhail. I know you know all I have done. This is why you are here. You cannot stop me. You must leave at once. Please go."

Mikhail closed his eyes. Carrie watched him ball his hands into tight fists. He looked like he had a strong desire to lash out at someone, anyone. She turned to Loren. "Don't you see how much you're hurting him?" she said. "I know you love your son. Why are you doing this to him?"

"I am not doing this *to* him," Loren cried out. He looked around as if afraid someone was listening in. "I am doing this *for* him. I got the mirror for the dybbuks, because they told me that after Asmodeus was defeated, no dybbuk could touch it. I was told that if I helped them they would not harm a single hair on my son's head. They were planning to get revenge on all of you. They got to you, Carrie, by taking your friends. They were going to do the same to you, Emilia. Your only friend here is my son. Mikhail, you are all I have left." Loren was sobbing, tears coursing down his cheeks. "I cannot lose you. As a parent, I did what I had to do to protect my child."

Carrie looked up into Mikhail's face and saw his expression soften. "Father," he said. "Do you not realize what they did? There are two young women trapped in that mirror. They are someone's children. Their parents do not know what has befallen them. Why must they suffer as you feared to?"

Loren sighed. Carrie could swear she could hear his heart breaking. "Please, sir," she said to him. "Those are my best friends. Please let me take them home to their parents."

Loren's eyes conveyed the warring emotions he was fighting. "But Mikhail," he said. "Who will protect my son?"

"I will," Emilia said tenderly. "I have assumed control over the dybbuks. I will ensure his safety."

Loren looked from Emilia to Carrie, and then he turned to Mikhail. "I am so sorry," he said to his son. "You must be so ashamed of me. The mirror is in Mikhail's bedroom."

As Loren stepped aside and Mikhail stepped forward, the fireplace exploded outward into the room. Flaming pieces of timber and stone showered Carrie and her friends. She heard screams as she, Emilia, and Mikhail were pelted by the smouldering shrapnel. Her previous injuries flared with a new pain, and a myriad of new places of agony clouded her mind. As she tried to pick herself up off the floor, a wail of despair and anguish ripped through the room. She turned to see Loren kneeling on the floor, his son, her precious Mikhail, cradled lifelessly in his arms.

Chapter Twenty-Nine:
Ha Metsye

White-hot rage burned through Carrie's veins. After Adom, she had sworn to herself that she would never lose anyone else to the dybbuks. Then they had taken Lindsay and Rebecca. Now Mikhail was lost to her forever. The pain forgotten, she stood on shaky legs and crossed over to Loren. The walls of the room had been blown to pieces. Every window was shattered. The place was a smouldering wreck. Carrie gingerly stepped through it, knelt with Loren, and looked into Mikhail's face. He appeared serene and peaceful. His head seemed untouched by the blast. She looked down his body. His torso had been peppered by pieces of metal. There had been a cauldron lightly simmering on the dying fire. She tentatively reached out two fingers and pressed them against his neck. She let out a relieved sob.

"He's alive," she said to Loren. When he did not respond, she reached up and grabbed his face in her hands. "He's alive," she repeated. "I felt a pulse. He has a heartbeat. There's still hope."

Loren looked at her disbelievingly. "Are you certain?"

"Yes," Carrie answered. She laughed nervously. "He's alive. We'll need to find him a doctor very soon."

"That will be difficult," a sneering voice said from somewhere behind Carrie.

She turned to find herself face to face with a dybbuk. His wrinkled visage was split by a mean-spirited smile. She felt the intense desire to strike him hard.

"My son," moaned Loren. "You promised you would not harm my son."

"I promised I would not harm a hair on his head," the dybbuk said cruelly. "As you can see, I have kept my word. His head is in perfect condition." He laughed at Loren's distress. "You were about to turn against us."

"No," Loren said. "I will do anything you ask. Let me find help for my son."

"It is too late for that, old man," the dybbuk said. "You have outlived your usefulness. I should kill you right here."

"You would not dare." Emilia spoke as she climbed her way out of the rubble. Her hair was wild, and her face was stained. Every inch of her clothing was torn and covered with ash and soot. She had never looked fiercer. "How dare you harm my friends?" she growled at the dybbuk. "How dare you undermine my authority? I am your princess. I have assumed power."

"Power that I do not recognize," the dybbuk said. "I do not answer to you."

"Then who, pray tell, do you answer to?" Emilia asked, the challenge strong in her tone.

"I answer to Asmodeus," the dybbuk snarled.

"My father is gone," Emilia retorted. "You therefore answer to his heir. That is I, Princess Emilia."

"I will never answer to a half-breed like you. Besides, your father is here," the dybbuk said, laughing.

"You lie," Emilia said.

Carrie watched the exchange with growing anxiety. She could see Emilia was caught off guard by the dybbuk's response. Could it be possible? Could Asmodeus be alive?

"When you and that pathetic creature defeated your father, he was trapped in the mirror, as we trapped your friends," the dybbuk explained. "You free your friends, you free your father. No way around that."

Emilia went pale under the layers of grime. "That is impossible," she said. "This is a lie."

"No," the dybbuk said. "I lured you here on purpose. When I bring about my king's freedom, I shall be the biggest hero. He shall reward me mightily!"

"No, he will not," Emilia said.

Carrie sensed the burning anger rising in her friend. She watched in horror as Emilia flicked her hand and sent the dybbuk careening violently into the remains of the fireplace. He squealed in pain as he bounced off the rough stones. She flung him head first through the front window and walked over to see where he landed.

"Nobody harms my friends and gets away with it," she hissed at him.

Carrie saw her raise her hand for another assault. "Emilia, stop!" Carrie called out to her.

Emilia turned to face Carrie. "Why?" she asked. "Do you realize that if his plan was for us to get the mirror all along, then he hurt Mikhail for sport?"

"Yes," Carrie answered. "I do. But what you're doing now makes you just as bad. What does this accomplish?"

"It makes me feel better," Emilia said bitterly.

"But it doesn't fix anything here," Carrie gently pointed out. "We need to see the mirror, and we need to help Mikhail. That is what matters now. This dybbuk is unimportant."

"You are right," Emilia sighed. "I am sorry. I lost my temper. In some ways, I am more my father's daughter than I care to admit."

Carrie smiled wanly. "I think we all inherit bits of our parents we can't stand," she said. "Now what do we do?"

Emilia turned to Loren. "Leave him here with us," she said. "We will care for him. Go fetch a doctor, and be quick about it."

Loren hesitated a moment before putting Mikhail gently on the ground. He gave his son one last sorrowful look before running out the door as fast as his legs could carry him. Carrie went over, but Emilia stopped her with a raised hand.

"I shall stay with him while you get the mirror," Emilia said. "I know you want to be with him, but as a dybbuk, I cannot touch the mirror. It must be you."

Carrie nodded and walked toward Mikhail's bedroom door. She took a deep breath and went inside.

Chapter Thirty:
Di Dibbuk Shpigl

Carrie pushed open the door to Mikhail's bedroom and cautiously crossed the threshold. She walked in slowly, looking around for any trace of the mirror. Everything about the room—the checked curtain on the window frame, the handmade quilt on the bed, the slim volume of poetry on the nightstand—suited who Mikhail was. Carrie was filled with worry for him. She prayed that Loren would be able to bring the doctor in time. She crouched down and peered under the bed, finding nothing but dust bunnies and a pair of shoes. She looked behind the wooden headboard and found nothing there either. Carrie saw a wardrobe sitting in the corner and walked over. She grasped the handle and pulled it open. Carrie was flooded with memories as she found herself face to face with Asmodeus' mirror. It was an item she was all too familiar with. Carrie could almost feel the heat, the blistering and burning of her hands as she stared at the round, gilded mirror that had once held the strings to Elijah's violin. She recalled grabbing it in Asmodeus' throne room and using it to deflect his cruel flames back in his direction. She shuddered at the memory and reached out a trembling hand to take it once more.

Carrie grasped the frame, almost surprised to find it cool to the touch. She lifted the mirror and found it to be much heavier than she remembered. Carrie looked at her reflection and was appalled to see her wild hair, the burn down her right arm, and the motley collection of bruises covering what she could see of her body. It appeared she had split her lip when the fireplace exploded, and there seemed to be a large bruise forming on her right cheekbone. She winced as she prodded it. Her eyes widened as she looked into the mirror. She could make out two figures approaching her from behind. Carrie turned her head to see who had entered the room but found herself to still be alone. She looked back at the mirror to see that the figures had come closer. Her eyes filled with tears of relief as she realized who they were. They walked faster as if they saw her there, and soon, the three girls were standing side by side in the mirror.

"Lindsay? Rebecca?" Carrie asked. "Can you hear me?"

"Yes, we can," Rebecca answered, her face filled with concern. "What happened to you?"

"It's a long story," Carrie said. She felt as if she wanted to laugh and cry all at once. She had thought she would never be able to speak to her friends again. "I'll tell you all about it when we get you out of there."

"'We'?" Lindsay asked. "Who's with you?"

"Emilia," Carrie answered. "And Mikhail." Her voice cracked when she said his name. Fresh worry coursed through her. She strained to hear if his father had returned with the doctor and heard no sign of it.

"Carrie," Lindsay said, looking concerned for her friend. "Are you okay?"

"No," Carrie honestly replied. "But I will be. Let's get you out of there. Okay?"

"Fine by me," Rebecca said. "This place is so creepy. I swear we've been hearing voices telling us we'll never get out. We almost started to believe them."

Carrie could see an odd mist start to form around her friends' feet. Something about it made her tense with fear. Her friends saw the look on her face and walked closer to her. The mist swirled around them as they moved easily through it.

"What is it?" Lindsay asked. "You seem freaked out."

"Can you see a weird mist all over the ground?" Carrie asked.

"Yeah," Rebecca answered. "This stuff keeps coming and going. I don't know what it is. It kinda weirds me out."

"Me, too," Lindsay added. "It's cold and creepy. I keep getting chills up my spine."

"How long have you guys been in there?" Carrie asked, filled with concern.

"I don't know," Rebecca answered. "It feels like hours."

Carrie was astonished. How was this possible? "Hours?" she asked. "You guys have been missing for two weeks!"

Rebecca gasped. "What?! But I had papers due, and a report to give. What am I supposed to do now?"

Lindsay looked at her friend in shock. "*That's* what you're worried about?" she asked. "I missed two weeks of rehearsal for a show I have a lead role in. How's this going to look for me?"

Carrie fondly watched her friends bicker. She was so relieved they were all right. "I'm going to take you guys into the main room," she said to them. "Emilia's there. We're going to find a way to get you out."

"Awesome," Lindsay said.

"Can't wait," Rebecca added.

Carrie lifted the mirror and left Mikhail's room. She crossed the floor of the cottage's main area, carefully picking her way through the charred bits of wood, metal, and rock to where Emilia knelt by Mikhail. Carrie felt her stomach twist into knots upon seeing him. He was far paler than he had been before she left.

"How is he?" Carrie asked, almost afraid to hear the answer.

"His condition has worsened," Emilia answered with tears in her eyes. "I do not know what to do to help him."

Carrie gently put the mirror down and knelt by Mikhail's side. She could hear him breathing laboriously, and took his hand in hers. "Mikhail?" she said, an audible tremor in her voice. "Can you hear me?" She looked up at Emilia. "Maybe some of the herbs he got in Shkalo can help him?"

Emilia shook her head. "I am not that skilled of a healer," she said. "If I knew the extent of his injuries, maybe."

"Mikhail," Carrie said once more. "I have the mirror. We at least have that going for us. I need you to wake up now. Okay?" She bent and placed a kiss on his cool lips. She sighed when nothing happened. "I don't know why I thought that might help. It always works in fairy tales."

"I have to believe he hears us," Emilia said. "He needs to know we have succeeded at least in part of what we hoped to achieve."

Carrie turned back to where the mirror lay. "It's the same one from your father's throne room," Carrie informed her. "What do we do?"

"Show it to me," Emilia said.

Carrie rose and picked the mirror up and held it out, facing the princess. She heard Emilia gasp and knew she could see their missing friends. She saw a chair nearby and leaned the mirror against it so they could both see what was happening in its reflection.

As if it had a sadistic sense of timing, the mist began to swirl violently around Rebecca and Lindsay's feet. Carrie and Emilia watched helplessly as it rose along their bodies, blanketing them in a grey fog. The two girls in the mirror cried out in fear, nearly blinded by the swirling, growing mist.

"Carrie!" Rebecca yelled. "It's alive! The mist is alive! It wants you to free us so it can get out. It's trapped here just like us."

"Oh my god!" Lindsay exclaimed, her voice full of terror. "Emilia, I'm hearing voices in the mist. It says it's your father! The mist is Asmodeus. It says that if you don't free us, we'll die!"

Chapter Thirty-One:
Behalah

"Emilia," Carrie said, panic creeping into her voice. "What do we do?" It was all too much. She felt as if she were breaking apart. Freeing her friends meant freeing Asmodeus. Leaving them there meant losing them forever. They still had not figured out how to even go about setting them free. On top of that, Loren had not returned with the doctor. "We can't leave them in there with him," she said to the princess.

"I know," Emilia said helplessly. "However, I am without ideas."

They sat and watched the mist grow thicker, almost obliterating their view of their friends. Carrie could hear from their cries that it was hurting them. She desperately wanted to clamp her hands over her ears, shut her eyes, and pretend none of this was happening.

"From what I can understand," Emilia said, "when you used the mirror to deflect my father's fire, it must have reflected it back at him destroying his corporeal form. He was then trapped in the item of his undoing."

"But that doesn't help us get my friends out," Carrie said. "Do you know any spells, charms, potions that can help?"

"No," Emilia said. "I am as helpless as you. Even more so since I cannot even touch the mirror."

Carrie jumped, startled as the door to the cottage was flung open. She turned and saw Loren run in, in a blind panic, followed closely by a thin woman wearing spectacles and greying hair pulled back in a bun. Emilia looked at the pair, relief written across her face.

"Doctor Rachel," Emilia gasped. "Mikhail is here. Can you help him?"

The doctor rushed over to her patient's side and began her examination, pulling his tunic aside. Carrie bit her lip hard to keep from crying out as she saw the extent of his injuries. His entire torso looked burnt and covered with gashes. She could not tell where one injury ended, and a new one began. Rachel pulled her bag open and began pouring liquids over his wounds, cleaning them so she could get a better look. Emilia left his side and went over to Carrie. She pulled her away.

"Let her work," Emilia said. "She is quite skilled. He could not be in better hands. We can do nothing for him now, so let us focus on saving Lindsay and Rebecca."

Carrie reluctantly nodded in agreement. "Okay," she said. "Do you have any ideas at all?"

Emilia grimaced. "One," she said, "but it is a last resort. If we do this, there is no going back. I hesitate to even mention it…"

"What is it?" Carrie asked.

"We break the mirror."

Carrie looked at her friend as if she had gone completely mad. "What?!" she said, shocked. "That's crazy. How can that possibly save them?"

"I know," Emilia said. "It does not seem practical, but it was all I could think of."

"Well, it's better than what I thought of," Carrie admitted.

"What did you think of?" Emilia asked.

"Nothing," Carrie answered. "Absolutely nothing."

The two girls looked at the mirror, their friends' figures completely obscured from view by the mist. They felt completely helpless to save them.

"Lindsay, Rebecca," Carrie called to the glass. "Can you still hear me?"

"Yes," came a muffled reply. "We can. Get us out of here!"

"We're trying," Carrie said. "Emilia wants to break the glass. We can't think of another plan. Will that work? Do you know? What can you sense from Asmodeus?"

"Oh, Carrie," came Lindsay's voice from within the mist. "He says that once he gets free, he will destroy you in the worst ways possible. He doesn't want you to break the mirror. He says we're all done for if you do."

Carrie felt chills up her spine. Her arms were covered in goose pimples. "What does he mean by that?" she asked. She was not sure she wanted to hear the answer.

"I think he wants you dead," came the response. "Carrie, I—I don't think you should set him free. I think Emilia's right. Break the mirror. It's for the best. Let us go."

Carrie wanted to scream in frustration. She felt everything she held dear was being ripped from her grasp. She turned to Emilia and saw her own feelings echoed in the princess' face. Carrie turned and went to go check on Mikhail. She saw frustration and sadness in the doctor's eyes and felt her heart break further. Loren was sitting in a chair, shoulders slumped in defeat and an endless river of tears streaming from his emerald eyes. She reached up and ran her hands through her hair, dislodging a pile of ash. She turned back to Emilia, who looked back quizzically.

"What more can he possibly take?" Carrie said brokenly. "My life?"

"This is what he desires. Yes. What do you want to do?" Emilia asked. She looked at the mirror. "I am torn. We figure out how to save them, we potentially destroy all. We break the mirror, Hadariah is safe, but we will probably lose our friends."

"Guys?" Carrie asked facing the mirror. "Are you okay in there?"

"Carrie!" a voice called back. "He's hurting us! Make it stop! You can't let him out. He's planning much worse for you and Emilia! Break the glass!"

Carrie gave a short scream of anger and frustration. Loren looked up from his vigil. He looked so guilty, Carrie found herself feeling sorry for him. She understood that he had only desired to keep his son safe. Try as she might, she could not fault him for that. She turned and walked out of the front door. Carrie paced the front garden. In the light of the setting sun, the world looked so peaceful. It was so hard to reconcile the beauty outside with the pain that lay just inside the cottage walls.

Carrie heard the door behind her open and close. She turned to see Emilia walk up to her. The way she moved, so tentative and stiff, along with the look in her eyes, showed Carrie that the princess was feeling just as much pain as she, both physically and emotionally. Carrie realized that Emilia cared for Lindsay and Rebecca, and she also stood to lose her childhood friend—her best friend. Carrie opened her arms, and Emilia gratefully allowed herself to be enveloped in a tight embrace. The two girls just stood and cried out their pain, frustration, fear, and sadness. Finally, they broke apart. Emilia looked to Carrie for some sign that she knew what to do.

"If the dybbuks knew how to get someone out of the mirror, your father would probably be free right now," Carrie said.

"He probably would be," Emilia agreed.

"Can you think of anyone who can come up with a way to help them?" Carrie asked.

"This mirror is made by dybbuk magic," Emilia said. "There is no one who can reverse it. Only a dybbuk can undo a dybbuk spell. Even though I am one, this is beyond anything I learned to do."

"So what do we do?" Carrie asked. She knew in her heart the only solution, but did not want to face it.

"I think our only choice is to break it," Emilia said in a shaky voice. "At first I thought that might free them, but I doubt that to be the case. I also believe it wrong to leave the mirror with our friends being tortured by my father."

Carrie looked up at the sky. She refused to believe this was happening. It all felt so wrong. She wished with all her heart and soul that this was another one of her nightmares, but the pain from all of her injuries told her that this was not the case. She sighed, resigning herself to the task that must be done. She told herself that she and Emilia would be the only ones that would feel the loss. The dybbuk's spell had already succeeded in wiping her friends from existence in her world. Yet this thought only deepened her pain. She took a deep breath, steeling herself for what she was about to say. "Okay," Carrie said, her voice thick with unshed tears. "Let's do it. Let's break the mirror." She felt she had no other option. This way would also ensure no one else would suffer the same fate as Lindsay and Rebecca.

Emilia bit her lip nervously. She looked at Carrie sorrowfully. "I am sorry to say this, Carrie, but because I am a dybbuk, I cannot touch it. This dreadful task falls to you. It must be you alone to destroy my father's mirror."

Chapter Thirty-Two:
Menupatz

Carrie was numb. She had forgotten all about Emilia's problem with the mirror. She had thought her friend would share the responsibility. She did not know if she could go through with this alone. She walked away, consumed by the desire to be alone. She did not want anyone near her at the moment. She just wanted to be alone with her thoughts. How could she do this? Was this really the only way? She felt so torn. She wanted so badly to be home with her parents. She wanted to be in class with her new friends. She wanted to be laughing and talking with Lindsay and Rebecca. She wanted to be anywhere but where she was.

A new image came to her mind. She remembered a day, what felt like eons ago. She remembered sitting in residence, a new boy sitting across from her telling her about how he had been sent by a princess. She remembered how the sunlight fell across his high cheekbones. How his grey eyes seemed to take in every inch of his surroundings, of her. Carrie hugged herself tightly, remembering how he looked when she last saw him, lying battered on the floor of his home.

Carrie remembered Lindsay walking through the giants' forest singing a song about rainbows from her childhood. A song of magic and hope. She remembered how happy she had looked, immersed in her music. She remembered her long, blonde hair swinging in the darkness, her blue eyes sparkling and happy. She remembered her friend content to be with those she cared about, no matter what the surroundings. Carrie then thought about her friend's fear and pain when she last heard her speak, begging her to break the mirror.

Carrie remembered Rebecca, smiling and laughing as they drove on one of their road trips, her dark eyes flashing in the sunlight, black hair pulled back in a ponytail. She remembered her friend joking, and taking pictures for her mother back home. Carrie bit back a sob realizing that soon she would be the only one capable of remembering any of these things about the two people who had been there for her for the past fifteen years of her life. She felt as if her heart was being ripped from her chest. She did not know if she could handle this.

She turned and looked back at the cottage. She longed to run and never look back, but she knew she could not do that. She still had Emilia—Emilia, who was going through the same amount of pain. Emilia might lose Mikhail as well. Emilia had also thought of Lindsay and Rebecca as friends. She would help Carrie remember. She would be there for her, as Carrie would in return.

Carrie steeled herself for what she felt she must do and headed back inside on shaky legs. She looked at Mikhail who had been moved from the floor to a long sofa, his head propped by pillows. Rachel had bandaged him as best she could. Carrie could see how pale he was, and she felt her heart break still further. Loren sat by his son's side, clutching his hand as if it were a lifeline. Mikhail's father looked utterly broken. Carrie added him to her mental list of Asmodeus' victims.

Carrie felt Emilia place a hand on her shoulder, and she nodded as if to tell her friend she was ready. She walked over to the mirror and lifted it as high as she could. She felt its weight in her hands, the coolness of its glass, and peered intently into the mist. Her hands were shaking from nerves and exertion. She looked to Emilia for encouragement and support. The glass was still obscured by the mist, but her friends were silent. Part of her wanted to call out to them, see if they were still nearby. Another part was certain that if she heard their voices again, she would not have the strength to carry through with this task. She made a motion as if to heave the mirror to the floor, and at the last second, she hesitated and put it back down.

"I can't," Carrie said. "I can't do this." She turned her tear-stained face to Emilia. "Is there a chance this will save them instead of destroy them?"

"I initially thought so, yes," Emilia said.

"Are you just saying that?" Carrie asked, a tiny sliver of hope in her voice.

Emilia did not say another word, merely shaking her head. Carrie took a deep breath. She lifted the mirror again, and this time she threw it with all her might against the cottage's stone floor, showering the space around Carrie and Emilia with a thousand shards of glittering glass. Carrie looked desperately at the place the mirror once stood and only saw an empty frame. Panic began to set in. What had she done? Carrie looked around the room. Nothing else had changed. She opened and closed her hands, feeling how empty they felt. Panic welled up in her chest, and she started breathing heavily.

"Emilia?" Carrie asked in a small voice, "what have I done?"

Familiar arms wrapped themselves around her as Emilia pulled her close. Carrie leaned back, feeling nothing. She had done it. She had actually done it.

"Girls," Rachel called from across the room.

Carrie pulled herself free from Emilia's grasp as she whirled around, fearing something horrible had happened to Mikhail. "What is it?"

"Look," Rachel said. She pointed a trembling finger toward the empty frame.

A swirling grey mist had started to form. It quickly doubled, then tripled in size. Carrie could feel her heart thumping painfully in her chest. As the mist grew, Carrie could see two shapes begin to appear. Her mouth went dry as she watched in shock. The figures slowly stood, and Carrie could see them clearly. She gave an involuntary cry of joy as she recognized her two friends.

Lindsay and Rebecca had been saved!

They turned and saw their friend and ran over to her, as the swirling mist began to gather and move about the room. Carrie found herself caught up in a much-desired group hug with Lindsay, Rebecca, and Emilia. Pulling away, Carrie saw the mist travel over to where Mikhail lay defenceless and realized with horror that Asmodeus had found his freedom as well.

Chapter Thirty-Three:
Der Ams Vire Fun Di Dibbux

Carrie was at a loss. She saw the mist waft its way over to where Mikhail, his father, and Rachel were huddled in fear, and felt frozen in place. She turned to Emilia, silently pleading for help, and the princess shook her head as if saying that she was out of ideas. Rebecca and Lindsay clutched Carrie's arms, terrified by what may happen.

"How do we stop him now?" Lindsay asked. "How can you stop something like smoke?"

"I don't know," Carrie said.

The mist gathered before them, forming a funnel cloud. It began to spin wildly, tossing pieces of rubble into the air. Carrie and her friends were forced to crouch down, shielding their faces from the onslaught. Carrie could swear she heard a man's voice cackling in her mind. She gritted her teeth, screwing her eyes shut as she felt her hair being whipped about her cheeks. She felt her friends' arms around her, and took a little comfort from the fact that they were together once more. She could feel small pieces of wood and broken glass hit her body, causing even more scratches and bruises. She kept herself from crying out in pain, not wanting to give Asmodeus the satisfaction. Carrie heard small whimpers from her friends and she reached out, taking their hands.

Almost as soon as it started, it was over. Carrie gingerly opened her eyes and took in the wreckage of the room. Whatever had been left untouched from the fireplace's explosion was now destroyed. The mist had vanished. The four girls picked themselves up off the floor, and Carrie immediately ran over to Mikhail. Rachel had covered him, using her body as a shield, from Asmodeus' attack. She met the doctor's eyes and saw relief there. Mikhail was still alive. Carrie turned to Loren and found he had left his chair. She saw him standing at the foot of the sofa, staring dispassionately at his son. Something about his posture made Carrie uneasy.

"Sir?" Carrie asked. "Are you okay?"

"Disgusting," Loren spat with a twist of his lip. "It pains me to see our word being sullied so."

Carrie took an involuntary step backwards. "Whose word?" she asked him.

"They use semantics to justify going back on a bargain," Loren continued as if he had not heard her. "The dybbuk that made the deal with this man will be dealt with harshly. He knew what the old man meant and had fun destroying him. If we do not have our word, we have nothing. No one will deal with us if this gets out."

"Asmodeus," Carrie said, understanding dawning on her. "You can restore the good faith people had."

Asmodeus looked up sharply. Loren's green eyes were unnaturally dark with anger. "What are you saying?" he snapped at her. "Give me one good reason I should listen to you. You are the reason I was in this predicament in the first place. I should crush you like the insect you are."

Carrie heard her friends behind her get up and come over to flank her on either side. She smiled sweetly at Asmodeus, trying hard to mask her fear. "You won't," she said, sounding a lot more confident than she actually felt.

"And why not?" Asmodeus drawled, a cruel smile on his lips.

"Because you owe me," Carrie said. "If it weren't for me, you would still be trapped in that mirror. It's because of me you're even standing here at all."

Asmodeus snorted in derision. "If it were not for you, I would not have been in the mirror in the first place," he pointed out.

Carrie waved her hand through the air as if this were trivial nonsense. "We could argue this 'til the cows come home," she said feigning indifference.

"What are you doing?" Rebecca hissed in her ear.

"Trust me," Carrie whispered back. She looked Asmodeus in the eye. "We could keep arguing for as long as we wanted. I released you, and you owe me. I propose a deal."

Asmodeus looked intrigued. "Oh really?" he asked, crossing his arms across his chest. "What sort of deal?"

"It's a deal where we both come out on top," Carrie said. She hoped her plan would work. She knew she was taking a fairly large gamble.

"Go on," Asmodeus said. He leaned back against the wall behind him, affecting an air of nonchalance.

"You heal Mikhail," Carrie said. "You restore him to perfect health, as if he had never been injured. This way, if people hear he was hurt by the dybbuk, they will also hear you honoured the deal with his father by fixing the situation. So it will restore faith in your word. I get my friend back, and we are square. I owe you nothing, and you owe me nothing."

Asmodeus cocked his head to the side, considering this suggestion. He casually waved his hand. "Done," he said. He looked Carrie in the eye. "Now we are 'square,' as you put it. I will still have my revenge on you. You wait and see about that." He turned to Emilia, who shrank back under her father's gaze. "As far as I am concerned, you are no longer my child," he said to her. "You gallivant with these humans who seek to destroy me. You turn against me and then try to usurp my power. I should crush you where you stand. I will not see you in my home ever again." He turned, waved a hand over Mikhail's body, and vanished from the cottage, leaving the four girls, Rachel, and Mikhail alone.

Carrie sank down onto the arm of the sofa. She realized she was shaking from head to toe. She looked up and truly saw her friends standing there, whole. She beamed up at them, tears in her eyes. She began to laugh, the tension leaving her body fully for the first time in weeks. Lindsay and Rebecca flung themselves into Carrie's arms, nearly knocking her off her perch.

"You're back," Carrie said. "You're really back. I thought I'd lost you for good."

"You can't get rid of us that easily," Lindsay said, laughing and crying into Carrie's shoulder.

"We knew you'd come for us," Rebecca said. "By the way, you guys look like you've been tossed through a meat grinder. What happened?"

"Long story," Carrie said. "I'll tell you everything later."

Lindsay and Rebecca unwound themselves from Carrie's arms and went to hug Emilia again. Carrie went to kneel by Mikhail's side. Rachel was slowly unwinding his bandages, exclaiming in shock as she went. Everywhere she looked; there was nothing but smooth, unblemished skin. Carrie could not help but smile. It had worked. Now she just needed him to wake up to confirm he was all right. Carrie took his hand in hers, not wanting to ever let go. She felt Rachel gently touch her face, and turned to find the doctor looking at her with mild concern in her eyes.

"I do not know when he will wake," Rachel said, "but while we wait, may I examine your injuries?"

Carrie reluctantly let go and turned herself over to the doctor's ministrations. Rachel then moved on to look over Emilia, Rebecca, and Lindsay, proclaiming them all bruised and battered but otherwise healthy. Carrie and Emilia took up positions by Mikhail once more, and Carrie found herself recounting their adventures to her friends, telling them both about Muzikonstin and the children they had befriended. Emilia took over the telling when Carrie reached the part where they went to Shkalo. Carrie took over once more to tell them about Mikhail and how he had kissed her, blushing furiously when she got to that part. Lindsay and

Rebecca listened in wonder when they heard about the shretele and how they had found the mirror. They were concerned when Carrie told them how she had been thrown off her horse, and became perplexed when they were told about how they had begged Carrie to break the mirror.

"We never said that," Lindsay told them. "We knew Asmodeus wanted you to break the mirror. He kept saying as much."

Emilia's eyes were dark with anger. "My father mentally tortured us to get his way," she snarled. She looked at Mikhail. "I pray he did not just restore the body. I hope he wakes soon."

Carrie turned to Mikhail. She could see he was breathing much easier than he had been previously. She remembered back to when he had helped her just outside of Muzikonstin. He told her that people could do magic if they believed strongly enough. She put her hand on his head. *I have faith he will be okay. I have faith he will come back to us. He will be all right.* She filled her mind with images of him laughing and smiling. She remembered how he had looked when he showed her how to start a fire with flint. She remembered his kiss in Shkalo's town square. *He will be okay.*

Emilia gave a small gasp of surprise, and Carrie opened her eyes. Mikhail was lying there staring up at them all. His grey eyes were free of pain, and when he saw Carrie looking down at him, he smiled brightly at her.

"Is it over?" he asked them. "Have we won?"

Carrie laughed and kissed him happily, not caring who saw or said anything about it. For the first time, she did not blush afterwards. "We got them back," she told him. She gestured to her friends. "Mikhail," she said, "this is Lindsay and Rebecca."

"Hi," her friends said to him.

Mikhail pulled himself into a seated position and looked around the room. "I remember the fireplace exploding," he said. "Everything after that is fuzzy. Where is my father?"

Emilia touched his arm to get his attention. "Mikhail," she said sadly, "I am so sorry. Asmodeus was trapped in the mirror with Lindsay and Rebecca. When they were freed, he was as well."

"Has he harmed my father?" Mikhail asked, his face filled with worry and fear.

"He has possessed him," Emilia said softly. "Asmodeus' body was destroyed when we saved Hadariah. He took your father's body as a replacement."

"So there's still a chance he may be saved," Mikhail said, grim determination colouring his voice.

"There is," Emilia said. "However, there is no telling where he may have gone."

Mikhail turned to her, eyes pleading. "You're his daughter," he said. "Surely you have *some* idea."

"I am his daughter no longer," she said sadly. "He has disowned me." She turned to Carrie. "I do not know why this upsets me. After all we have done to each other, it still hurts."

Mikhail took her hand in his. "I understand," he said. "We may not like what our parents do. We may disagree with them. Yet, they are still our parents. What they do still affects us."

Emilia nodded in agreement. "This is quite true," she said, pulling him into a tight hug. "I am so happy to have you back, my friend."

Rachel walked around the room, collecting whatever supplies were still salvageable. "I am glad you are all okay," she said. "I am going to leave you now. I must return home to my family."

"Thank you for all you have done," Mikhail said sincerely. "I am sorry for everything."

"It is not your fault," Rachel told him. "I will see you soon."

Mikhail watched her leave and surveyed the damage done to his home. "What am I going to do?" he asked. "I cannot stay here. I do not even think I want to anymore."

"Pack what you want and come to the palace with me," Emilia said. "I am sure the king and queen will give you a place to stay."

Mikhail looked gratefully at his friend. He nodded and silently went to go pack his things.

The four girls sat together on the sofa. Lindsay and Rebecca sat on either side of Carrie, leaning on her shoulders.

"Now that this is all over," Rebecca said. "Will the king and queen open the ways between worlds again? You told us they had been closed."

"Yeah," Lindsay added. "It'll be pretty hard for Carrie and Mikhail to have a relationship if they can't visit each other."

Carrie playfully poked Lindsay in the side eliciting a laugh from her friend. She was happy that everything between them seemed fine.

"I think that will be done," Emilia said.

"Good," Rebecca replied. "I missed you. It would be nice to be able to see each other as well—Carrie's love life aside."

Emilia laughed. "I missed you as well," she told her. "I should like to see your world. You have told me so much about it."

Mikhail exited his room, a burlap sack flung over his shoulder. "I am ready to go," he said. He headed to the front door, barely looking back at what was left of his childhood home.

Carrie and her friends got up off the sofa and followed him out the front door. In the yard, Mikhail turned and gave his home one last look before sighing and leading the way back to the palace.

Chapter Thirty-Two:
Ha Armon

They returned to the palace following the shortcuts that Emilia and Mikhail led them through. With no stops in any towns or villages, the trip did not take very long. Lindsay and Rebecca marvelled at the speed, realizing quickly that the first time they had been there the false Emilia had been taking them the long way around.

They reached the palace just at sunset on the second day of their journey, the setting sun bathing the palace in a fiery light, casting the towers in hues of orange and red. As they passed through the main gate, the palace servants ushered everyone into separate rooms to be bathed and pampered before being given an audience with the king and queen.

Clad in a deep-blue gown trimmed with ermine, Carrie walked into the throne room feeling clean and refreshed. Lindsay and Rebecca were already present, scrubbed clean and both dressed in deep purple. She smiled happily at her friends, hardly daring to believe that she had them back. She ran over to them, clutching their birthday gifts in her hand. She had decided while getting ready to give them to them early.

"I know it's not your birthdays yet," Carrie said. "I wanted you to have these now, though."

Lindsay and Rebecca took the silver chamtzahs and smiled widely.

"I love it," Lindsay said putting hers around her neck.

"It's perfect," Rebecca told Carrie as she put hers on as well. "Thank you."

"You're so welcome," Carrie said, hugging each of her friends in turn.

Emilia and Mikhail walked into the room together, Emilia resplendent in a forest green gown, Mikhail wearing brown pants and a navy tunic. Upon seeing Carrie, Mikhail strode forward quickly, scooping her up in his arms.

"I have been told I may stay here," he whispered in her ear.

"I'm glad," Carrie told him. It warmed her heart knowing he had a place where people cared about him.

The king and queen entered the room, taking their places on the thrones. Rebecca and Lindsay murmured excitedly to each other upon seeing that the queen was with child. They all bowed and curtseyed to the royal couple and waited to hear what they had to say.

"I want to extend our thanks for your services rendered in aiding the citizens of not only Muzikonstin, but also Shkalo," the king said. "I have been told that Asmodeus is once more free and roaming Hadariah. We have increased the protection around Elijah's violin. Hopefully this will deter another attack."

"I have spoken with my husband," the queen said. "We have agreed to leave the ways between worlds open. Closing them helped no one, and it would be a pity to prevent our champions from visiting our world."

Carrie and Mikhail exchanged relieved smiles. Lindsay and Rebecca both thanked the royal couple and began to talk excitedly about a future visit. Suddenly, Rebecca looked concerned.

"Your majesty," Rebecca said to the king. "I've been told that we were missing for at least a few weeks. I have responsibilities at home. My absence will put me in a very bad situation with several people. Is there a way to fix this?"

"Tell me what you need," the king said to her with a kind smile.

"I don't know," Rebecca said. "I need a way to convince my professors that I was not slacking off. I need to tell them that I was seriously unable to attend class and write my papers. However, I don't think telling them I was kidnapped by magical creatures will be much help."

"Me, too," Lindsay said. "I'm in a similar situation."

The king nodded in understanding. "You just leave this in my hands," he assured them. "It will be taken care of. You have my word."

Rebecca and Lindsay looked relieved. They thanked the king, and he and the queen left the room, leaving the five friends together. They roamed the grounds in a tight group, Rebecca and Lindsay getting to know Mikhail by peppering him with questions and proclaiming him 'suitable' for Carrie, much to his embarrassment. They filled Emilia in on all they had been up to, and Lindsay got a promise from her to come and watch her perform in her next show. Carrie was mostly silent, just enjoying the feel of Mikhail's hand in hers and the endless chatter of her friends. After all they had been through, it was wonderful knowing that things had mostly turned out fine.

Carrie took a moment to visit Adom's grave. She knelt by the small cluster of stones, adding one of her own to the growing monument. She whispered a tender thanks to her friend and rose to find that everyone had joined her. They too knelt, placing rocks atop the mound, sharing in a moment of silence before moving on.

The Song of Vengeance

It was late evening when they met the king and queen in the garden once more. The king reinforced the fact that they could stay as long as they wished, but they knew that with all their responsibilities back home, it was simply impossible. Carrie exchanged glances with Mikhail and Emilia, not wishing to leave them, but knowing that she must. She hugged the princess tightly, thanking her for her help in saving their friends and telling her to come visit whenever she could and as often as she wished.

She turned to Mikhail and took him in her arms. "I am so sorry about your dad," she whispered. "We will find a way to save him."

"I know," he said to her. "If anyone can help him, I believe it is you."

"Come and see me soon," she told him. "I'll miss you."

"I will miss you, too," he said. He kissed her deeply. "This is not goodbye. This is until we meet again."

Carrie nodded, not trusting her voice. She saw Rebecca and Lindsay take turns saying goodbye to Emilia, and laughed as they both grabbed Mikhail in a hug. She knew that he was accepted as a part of their group, and was glad of it. The king and queen then led them to a stone archway.

"This arch will take you wherever you need to go," the queen said. "Simply picture your destination in your mind, and that is where you will end up. Once you leave, we will be placing it under guard to try and give you some protection in your world."

"Thank you for everything," Carrie told them. "We appreciate it all."

"You are very welcome, Carrie," the queen said, with a warm smile.

Carrie turned back and waved at Emilia, Lindsay, Rebecca, and Mikhail, giving herself one last look at them before stepping through, an image of her residence planted firmly in her mind.

Chapter Thirty-Five:
Tsurik Tsu Fakt

It had been three days since she had come home. Every day, she'd spoken to Lindsay and Rebecca for hours. Somehow, all their papers had been turned in on time, and Rebecca's professor had given her a ninety percent on a presentation she had never given. Lindsay's director had remembered her being at every single rehearsal. Despite the fact that things had worked out in their favour, they found the whole situation very unnerving. Carrie went to dinner with her parents and was both relieved and disturbed to find that neither of them even recalled their last argument. She told them about Mikhail, and they insisted on meeting him. She promised she would arrange something the next time he came in for a visit. But so far, he had not come.

Carrie hung up her phone after saying goodbye to Lindsay. Her production of *Chess* was next weekend, and she'd made Carrie promise to come see it. She looked at her calendar and sighed. With all the homework she had to do, she thought it an impossible task to add a trip to Boston to her list of things to do. Furthermore, she was flat broke. *Why did I agree to this?* she asked herself. She shook her head, exasperated. She would have to call Lindsay back and make her apologies. It was not going to happen.

"Hey there," Amanda called from just outside the door.

Carrie turned and gave her neighbour a friendly wave.

"You look stressed," Amanda told her. "What's up?"

"My friend Lindsay made me promise to go and see her perform," Carrie said with a small frown.

"Ah," Amanda said. "But you told me she was good! Surely the show won't suck too badly."

Carrie smiled at Amanda remembering Lindsay. "The problem is that the show is in Boston, and it's next week," she explained. "I'm broke and have three papers due."

"Oh," Amanda said, screwing up her face in sympathetic frustration. "Sucks to be you I guess."

"Thanks," Carrie sarcastically replied.

"Come out for coffee," Amanda said. "It'll make you feel better."

"Broke. Remember?" Carrie pointed out.

"I'll pay," Amanda said in a sing-song voice.

"You're a terrible influence," Carrie said laughing. "I might join you later. I should probably call her back and tell her I can't go after all."

"Okay," Amanda said. "I'll hold you to that." She turned and left, calling out greetings to her friends inviting them to join her.

Carrie looked back at her phone and sighed. She heard a soft cough from behind her and spun around in her chair in fright. Her eyes went wide as she saw Mikhail sitting on her windowsill wearing the same outfit he'd been when she had first seen him in her tutorial. "Mikhail!" she exclaimed, jumping up from her chair and throwing her arms around him.

He laughed and hugged her tightly. "I missed you," he said, lightly stroking her hair.

"Where have you been?" she asked him.

"I could ask you the same thing," he pointed out. "Things have been busy. We have been searching for Asmodeus, but he seems to be in hiding. There has been no sign of him."

"How are you holding up?" Carrie asked him. She reached up to touch his face, and he leaned into her hand.

"I miss my father," he said. "Some days are harder than others. The king has decided to keep me busy. He has made me apprentice to the palace bard. I am learning to be a proper poet. Maybe soon, my verse will not be so terrible."

"I'd love to hear some," Carrie said, her eyes shining with happiness.

"Soon," he promised. "What has been happening with you?"

"My parents want to meet you," she said. "I've decided to change my major again—I applied to the visual arts program to focus on my painting. I have what feels like a million papers due, and I am about to disappoint a friend." She frowned at the phone as if it were somehow its fault.

"I would love to meet your parents," Mikhail told her. "Your art is wonderful. This seems like the best place for you. But why are you going to disappoint someone?"

"Lindsay invited me to her show next weekend, and I can't afford the trip," she said. "Even if I could, there's no time. I told you, I have all this work to do."

"Maybe think differently about the problem," Mikhail said.

"What do you mean?" Carrie asked bewildered.

"Travel to Hadariah and use the archway to go to Lindsay," he explained. "You can only be gone for the one night and still be able to have time for your work. It will also cost you nothing. That's how Emilia is going to watch her performance."

Carrie grinned up at him. "My boyfriend is so smart," she said with a laugh. "So you really want to meet my parents?"

"Yes," he told her. "I really do."

"How about dinner this weekend?"

"It is a date," he said. "Rebecca taught me that expression," he explained seeing the laughter in her eyes.

"She told me she went to visit Emilia," Carrie said. "I'll call my mom and set it up. Does seven work for you?"

"Whatever you want," he told her.

"Hmm…" She leaned in and kissed him. "How about that?"

"Perfect," he told her with a smile.

"I was going to go for coffee with some friends," she said to him. "Would you like to come with me?"

"I would love to," he said. "Though I thought you said you had work to do."

"I am a master procrastinator," she informed him. "I'll probably be up at three in the morning pounding away on my computer. But I'll get it done."

Mikhail shook his head at her. "I love you. Did you know that?"

Carrie's breath caught in her throat. This was the first time a boy had said this to her. She stood staring at him. "I…I love you too."

Mikhail looked so relieved. Carrie almost thought he'd been worried she wouldn't say it back. She held out her hand. "Shall we?"

"Of course," he said, pulling her closer.

As they walked to the coffee shop, Carrie smiled, finally feeling content. Asmodeus could wait. Her papers could wait. She was going to enjoy this moment for all it was worth.

Epilogue

Asmodeus stood and glared at himself in the mirror.

Through borrowed eyes, he looked himself up and down. He mentally snarled at the pleading voice in his head. Freedom would not be granted. At least, not yet.

He still had much to do. He continued his survey of Loren's body and sneered at his reflection. Pathetic. What he saw before him filled him with loathing. He was severely irritated that he could change nothing. His eyes that could once inspire fear in the hearts of men now were dull and filled with the pathetic trappings of humanity. He longed for his powerful build and his ability to change his shape with a mere thought. This body was so ordinary and human—it disgusted him.

He consoled himself with the thought that this would not last long. This situation was temporary. Soon, he would return to his former state of glory and power. Soon, the human girl and her friends would pay. His treacherous daughter would pay. And when they did, when he was himself again, this world would burn.

Be sure to watch for the final book in the *Dybbuk Scrolls Trilogy*,
The Song of War

Acknowledgements

As always, I would like to thank my team of extraordinary pandas for helping me make this book what it is. Thank you Rachel and Heather for your hard work editing my words. Thank you Don for creating the amazing cover, and a heartfelt thank you to Zara for believing in this story. Thank you to my family for believing in me and for putting up with the long hours of writing, rewriting, edits and research. This story is for you, but it is especially for my bubbie Helen.

Growing up in Czechoslovakia, and later Poland, my bubbie and her friends achieved what few young women did at the time and went to university. My bubbie studied business, and her best friend Lola pursued her dream and became a doctor. They believed that life would continue as it always had. They would fall in love, get married and have a family. Lola did that, just as things started to look bleak for the Jewish people in 1940's Poland.

In 1940, Poland was divided up between Germany and Russia. My bubbie found herself under Stalin's rule, and was soon part of Stalin's mass deportations and was sent away to a forced labour camp in Siberia with her mother and three of her brothers. Her father and brother Nathan stayed behind. She would never see them again. They managed to evade capture by the Russians, but was later caught by the Nazis and beaten to death. Lola stayed in Poland practising medicine, believing that her blond hair and blue eyes would keep her safe from the danger that was all around her. As long as people believed she was a gentile, and continued to practise medicine, she considered herself safe. Over the course of the Second World War, my bubbie's life was anything but easy. However her inner strength and faith that things would somehow get better kept her going.

My bubbie would tell me stories about this time in her life if I prompted her. She would tell me how they were always cold, how there was never enough food. She told me how her brother Marek ran away to join the resistance but was brought back. My mind was filled with these true stories of her life, and every day I thank God that she persevered and survived.

About the Author

Alisse Lee Goldenberg holds a Bachelor of Education and a fine arts degree; she has studied fantasy and folklore since she was a child. Alisse lives in Toronto, Canada, with her husband, Brian, and their triplets Joseph, Phillip, and Hailey. This is her second novel in the *Dybbuk Scrolls Trilogy*. She is also the author of the *Sitnalta Series* as well as the *Bath Salts Series*, which is co-authored by An Tran. Please feel free to visit her at www.alisseleegoldenberg.com.

My Bubbie and two of her friends in pre-war Poland. Gisa is on the left, marked with a 'G,' and Helen, my Bubbie, is in the centre.

Glossary

behalah. Panic (Hebrew).

boker. Morning (Hebrew).

chamtzah. Also known as the Hand of Fatima. It is a talisman used to ward off the evil eye. It resembles a hand with an eye in the middle (Hebrew).

chaverim. Friends (Hebrew).

der ams vire fun di dibbux. The true ruler of the dybbuks (Yiddish).

di dorf. The village (Yiddish).

Di Dibbuk Shpigl. The Dybbuk's Mirror (Yiddish).

dybbuk. A demon. Sometimes the soul of a dead person that has the ability to possess the living (Yiddish).

erev. Evening (Hebrew).

eyfo aten. Where are you? (Hebrew).

geyeg. Hunting (Yiddish).

gilgl. The spirit of a deceased person who refuses to accept that they have died (Yiddish).

ha armon. The palace (Hebrew).

ha derech. The way, or path (Hebrew).

hashiva ha baytah. Homecoming (Hebrew).

hu lo amar. He did not say (Hebrew).

iberrashn gast. Surprise guest (Yiddish).

imut. Confrontation (Hebrew).

Kapelyushniklech. A small dwarf-like creature that loves playing pranks. Has an odd affinity to horses (Yiddish).

khaloymes ve sfeykes. Dreams and doubts (Yiddish).

konflikt. Trouble (Yiddish).

lante. A bridge-dwelling goblin like creature. Waylays travellers using riddles (Yiddish).

Leygn aroyf baryerz, haltn ir zikher. Suf di tsores, shtum vos iz dort. Put up barriers, keep her safe. End the suffering, mute what is there (Yiddish).

mefuchedet. Spooked/scared (Hebrew).

mishteh. Party (Hebrew).

nakht. Night (Yiddish).

nedarim. Absent (Hebrew).

Shaliach. Emissary (Hebrew).

shretelech. Plural. A small elf-like creature that will help humans in exchange for gifts (Yiddish).

shtot bagegenish. Town meeting (Yiddish).

tsayt meshugas. A crazy time (Yiddish).

tshuvot. Answers (Hebrew).

tsurik tsu fakt. Back to reality (Yiddish).

vartn far nakht. Waiting for night (Yiddish).

vidertref. Reunion (Yiddish).

ziese. Sweetie (Polish).

Thank you for purchasing this copy of **The Song of Vengeance**. If you enjoyed this book, please let the author know by posting a review.

Growing good ideas into great reads…one book at a time.

Visit www.pandamoonpublishing.com to learn more about other works by our talented authors.

Mystery/Thriller/Suspense

- *122 Series Book 1: 122 Rules* by Deek Rhew
- *A Flash of Red* by Sarah K. Stephens
- *A Tree Born Crooked* by Steph Post
- *Fate's Past* by Jason Huebinger
- *Juggling Kittens* by Matt Coleman
- *Knights of the Shield* by Jeff Messick
- *Looking into the Sun* by Todd Tavolazzi
- *The Moses Winter Mysteries Book 1: Made Safe* by Francis Sparks
- *On the Bricks Series Book 1: On the Bricks* by Penni Jones
- *Southbound* by Jason Beem
- *The Juliet* by Laura Ellen Scott
- *Rogue Alliance* by Michelle Bellon
- *The Last Detective* by Brian Cohn
- *The New Royal Mysteries Book 1: The Mean Bone in Her Body* by Laura Ellen Scott

Science Fiction/Fantasy

- *Bath Salts Series Book 1: Bath Salts* by Alisse Lee Goldenberg and An Tran
- *Becoming Thuperman* by Elgon Williams
- *Dybbuk Scrolls Trilogy Book 1: The Song of Hadariah* by Alisse Lee Goldenberg

- *Dybbuk Scrolls Trilogy Book 2: The Song of Vengeance* by Alisse Lee Goldenberg
- *Everly Series Book 1: Everly* by Meg Bonney
- *.EXE Chronicles Book 1: Hello World* by Alexandra Tauber and Tiffany Rose
- *Fried Windows in a Light White Sauce* by Elgon Williams
- *Revengers Series Book 1: Revengers* by David Valdes Greenwood
- *The Crimson Chronicles Book 1: Crimson Forest* by Christine Gabriel
- *The Crimson Chronicles Book 2: Crimson Moon* by Christine Gabriel
- *The Phaethon Series Book 1: Phaethon* by Rachel Sharp
- *The Sitnalta Series Book 1: Sitnalta* by Alisse Lee Goldenberg
- *The Sitnalta Series Book 2: The Kingdom Thief* by Alisse Lee Goldenberg
- *The Sitnalta Series Book 3: The City of Arches* by Alisse Lee Goldenberg

Women's Fiction

- *Beautiful Secret* by Dana Faletti
- *The Long Way Home* by Regina West
- *The Mason Siblings Series Book 1: Love's Misadventure* by Cheri Champagne
- *The Mason Siblings Series Book 2: The Trouble with Love* by Cheri Champagne
- *The Mason Siblings Series Book 3: Love and Deceit* by Cheri Champagne
- *The Shape of the Atmosphere* by Jessica Dainty
- *The To-Hell-And-Back Club Book 1* by Jill Hannah Anderson

Made in the USA
Columbia, SC
22 January 2018